CHARM SCHOOL

A WITCHES THREE COZY MYSTERY

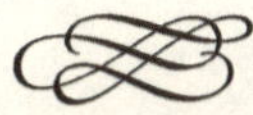

CATE MARTIN

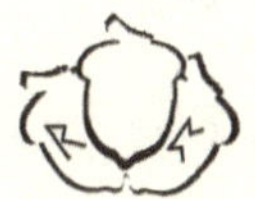

Cover design by Shezaad Sudar.

Cover images by Aarows, Yevheniia Bondarets and Stevloduv via Dreamstime.com.

Ratatoskr Press logo by Aidan Vincent Kise.

ISBN 978-1-946552-85-3

❀ Created with Vellum

CHAPTER 1

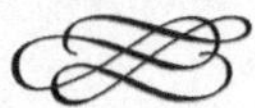

My name is Amanda Clarke, and I have a secret.

But I'm not sure how to describe it.

It's not like I can see the future or anything, and I wouldn't call it luck, but sometimes I wake up in the morning, and I just have a feeling about something. A strong, not to be argued with feeling that I either have to do something or absolutely cannot do something. I've never *not* obeyed that feeling, not even once.

Take, for instance, a perfectly ordinary Monday morning last April. I woke up an hour before my alarm was set to go off with a strong urge to go into work. I got dressed in my server's uniform and headed out my apartment door without even making any coffee or grabbing a bite of toast. I walked the couple of blocks from my building to the diner that has been the focal point of my entire life, my mother's workplace before it was mine, and let myself in the back door.

And found Mr. Schneiderman, the man who was like a grandfather to me, collapsed on the kitchen floor.

Heart attack. The paramedics said I saved his life. I wouldn't have found him in time if I hadn't woken up early and headed straight to the diner. Mrs. Schneiderman had been visiting her sick sister, and he had been alone.

Or that cold winter morning my senior year of high school when I had woken up with the certainty that I should call in sick to school, although I felt fine. Just before noon, as I was huddled in a nest of blankets watching *Titanic* for the umpteenth time, my mother had given a cry of alarm and staggered out of the kitchenette to collapse on the couch beside me.

Brain aneurysm. There was nothing I could do to save her. Maybe that's why I don't call these feelings any kind of luck. But I was there to hold her hand as the light faded from her eyes. I was the last thing she ever saw. I'm grateful to the powers that be, the ones who send the feelings, that I didn't go to school that day. That my mother didn't die alone.

But the strongest feeling I ever had didn't have a clear-cut beginning. It seemed to grow, pretty much from the day my mother died over the four and a half years until the day Cynthia Thomas entered the diner and my life.

The beginning may have been vague, but the feeling was not. It was very clear in my mind. Under no circumstances would I leave my hometown of Scandia, Iowa.

No one thought anything of it when I quit the traveling hockey team. My mother had just died, and the season was winding down with no shot at any playoff wins since all of our best players had graduated the year before.

And it didn't strike anybody as odd when I stayed on at my diner job. I had applied to a few colleges before she had died, but I didn't even bother opening the letters that came back. I wouldn't have been able to afford it, anyway.

And not leaving after that wasn't odd either. I was saving every penny I earned with the hope of someday soon having enough to get a trailer of my own in the park on the edge of town.

But even if anyone had asked me, I wouldn't have admitted that I just had a feeling. Scandia, as the name probably suggests, is populated with the descendants of Scandinavian immigrants, dairy farmers mostly. They are practical people, stoic, logical.

I can imagine the looks I'd get from the regulars at the diner if I admitted to even having these feelings, let alone letting them dictate my life.

Strangely, the most impulsive decision I ever made, the one prompted by Cynthia Thomas the day she appeared in the diner and took a table like any other customer off the highway, wasn't based on a feeling. Quite the opposite.

When Cynthia had finished her patty melt, leaving most of her fries but drinking six cups of coffee, her eyes never leaving me as I worked all my other tables, she waved me over. Thinking she was in a hurry, like most off the highway were, I already had her ticket ready.

Instead, I found myself looking at a cream-colored business card with Cynthia Thomas, Attorney, embossed on it.

I sort of heard what she was saying, but it was like listening to someone talking on a boat while your head's underwater. Something about a Miss Zenobia Weekes who had recently passed, and how her will had been very clear that I must be present at the reading. And the reading had to take place at midnight on the next full moon.

I know, weird. But I didn't think anything of it at the time.

Because I was too distracted by the sudden feeling of freedom. I hadn't even realized I wasn't free until just then. But it was like I had been shackled, both ankles, with balls and chains, like in the old cartoons. And now I wasn't.

I could leave Scandia.

I could go anywhere.

But Cynthia Thomas had handed me a thick envelope filled with traveling money and a map to Miss Zenobia Weekes' Charm School for Exceptional Young Ladies on Summit Avenue in St. Paul, Minnesota.

I had played hockey there once or twice, or rather in some of its suburbs. It was a pretty city. As good a place as any to see some of the world outside of Scandia. Because I still wanted that trailer to myself, and this trip was being paid for by the estate of Miss Zenobia Weekes.

How could I say no?

That was a month ago. Since then I've had more time to think, and yeah, the few details of the will I know are strange. And I'm not even sure why I, of all people, am being summoned to the reading. Cynthia couldn't—or wouldn't—tell me why. She said it would be clear at the reading.

She did tell me, when I asked, that Miss Zenobia Weekes wasn't a relative of mine. Which might seem like an odd question to ask a stranger, so let me explain.

I was born in the diner parking lot. My mother and the man who must have been my father were in a car going far too fast down the road in a sleet storm. He had hit a patch of ice and spun into a utility pole. By the time Mr. And Mrs. Schneiderman had gotten outside, he had been dead. My mother looked dead too, unconscious and bleeding from a blow to the head, but she jerked awake at Mr. Schneiderman's touch.

Then she went into labor. The nearest hospital was several miles down the highway, and I was born before the ambulance could make it there.

My entire life, my mother never spoke a word. She never wrote a word, either. She understood when others were talking and could nod or shake her head, but she largely preferred not to.

I don't know her name. My father had been wearing a work uniform with the name Clarke written on the breast pocket. Mr. and Mrs. Schneiderman named me Amanda when I was about three months old.

My mother worked in the kitchen at the diner and took care of me just fine. But she could never tell me anything about where she came from or who our people were.

But somehow this Miss Zenobia Weekes must have known her, because she certainly hadn't known me. I would've remembered a name like that.

And if I was nervous at all at attending the reading of a will at midnight on September's full moon, I just remembered Cynthia Thomas. She hadn't looked like someone up for summoning spirits or engaging in bloody sacrifices. She had looked exactly like what her business card said she was: a lawyer. Slacks and nice shoes, a business jacket over a cream-colored blouse. Not showy—she wasn't a corporate lawyer (if she had been, I probably would have had a different impression of her likelihood to be mixed up in sacrifices)—but clearly expensive, especially compared to the normal Scandia crowd around her.

But more than that, she had been kind. I had seen it in her blue eyes, in the wrinkles that a lifetime of soft smiles had etched into her skin. I had heard it in the tenor of her voice and the way she kept calling me "Miss Amanda." I had felt it when she had taken my hand just before leaving, a handshake that had lingered affectionately although we had just met.

I didn't know who Miss Zenobia Weekes was, but hearing the reverence in Cynthia's voice every time she said her name, I knew she had been someone very special. I was sure to learn more about her when I visited her school.

And I tried to not get my hopes up about the reading of a will. I was getting a free trip to a nice city, and a free stay in a house on the fanciest street in that city. That was treat enough for me.

But another part of me felt like all of that time I had spent trapped in my hometown, I had been waiting for something amazing.

And now that amazing thing was about to happen.

CHAPTER 2

The problem with being from a small town in northwestern Iowa is that it's really hard to leave it if you don't own a car. My mother had never driven, and I had never even learned.

Another one of those things about me no one ever found weird. I guess when you're born in the car crash that kills your father and probably damaged your mother's brain in a permanent way, it's not crazy to decide you never want to drive.

But mostly, since I could walk to work in less than five minutes, and could walk to the grocery store in less than ten, I never saw the point. That, and the expense of it all. I doubted I would have anything left to save of my wages and tips if I had subtracted out gas and insurance money, let alone the cost of an actual car.

So getting out of town, even with a thick envelope of cash, was tricky. But Mr. Schneiderman arranged it all for me. He was still too weak from his heart attack in the spring to drive even so far as Sioux Falls, but he knew pretty much everyone in town, and they all owed him favors. He found someone that was heading that way to deal with a legal matter and who agreed to give me a lift to the bus station.

It took eight hours to get to St. Paul. The less said about the bus trip, the better. I've had happier days. And I nearly got lost trying to get from the bus station to the local bus that would take me across the river from Minneapolis into St. Paul. But I didn't panic. I had Cynthia's card in my bag (the only bag I owned, the one that used to carry my books in high school, now stuffed with a few changes of clothes and my toothbrush); if worse came to worst, I could just call her, and she could pick me up.

But I'd rather arrive on my own.

I got off the bus in front of the cathedral in St. Paul. Somehow, its height was more moving than the skyscrapers of Minneapolis. My eyes just kept going up and up, following the ever narrower tapering of its spire as it stabbed up into the deep blue sky.

I'm sure they have ones in Europe that are more impressive, but it seemed unlikely I'd ever see any of those. I wondered how old it was, how much history had it seen pass by right where I was standing?

Did they still ring the bells? Would I be able to hear them from where I would be staying? What a lovely way to wake up in the morning, to the sound of bells tolling.

When I finally stopped staring up at the cathedral and found my way to Summit Avenue, I was blown still further away. Every building around me looked like it had been there for a century or more. And they were all so huge.

My hometown was a cluster of buildings at a crossroads just off the highway, and not a major highway at that. I lived in a tiny box of an apartment, just two rooms, and that's with counting the bathroom as its own room.

But now here I was, walking along a wide sidewalk past lovingly maintained yards and gardens, looking up at grand stone mansions built by the lumber barons and railroad men of another century. The building my apartment was in was only a few decades old, and it was already falling apart all around me and the other tenants. But these places looked like they could happily stand for centuries more and still be worth millions.

I was gawking too much and walking too slow, I realized as a man jogging with a dog had to stray out onto someone's lawn to get around me.

"Sorry!" I said, hugging my bag closer to my side and getting out of the middle of the sidewalk. I didn't think he could hear me with those earbuds in, but he glanced back at me with a smile in his green eyes and flashed me a thumbs up. He looked like he wanted to say something, but the Irish setter whose leash was tied around his waist suddenly picked up the pace, and he was compelled to do the same.

It was time to figure out where exactly I was going. I pulled my phone out of my back pocket.

It was the most expensive thing I owned, a first generation smartphone I had gotten refurbished at a terrific bargain.

I wouldn't call it a steal. But that word might be more appropriate than I'd like to think about. I didn't ask a lot of questions.

Since I usually got everywhere by foot and never left my hometown, I hadn't had the need to use the map feature ever before. Now I was discovering, in addition to its other little eccentricities of age, my phone's GPS was perhaps a bit subpar.

I squinted at the screen, then looked up at the buildings around me. There was no way I was in the right place, was there?

Then I remembered Cynthia Thomas in her expensive yet not flashy clothes. Cynthia Thomas definitely belonged in this neighborhood.

I looked again at the address, then looked up at the surprisingly modern-looking building in front of me. Condos. I could just see the view beyond the building, overlooking the valley and the Mississippi River as it swept past St. Paul for points further south. Even the condos must cost millions.

The house number was too high. I had gone too far. I frowned at the phone, which was telling me I had arrived at my destination. I poked at the screen until I made the street view appear. Perhaps if I saw what the front of the building looked like, I would have an easier time finding it.

The street view filled the screen. Quite literally in this case, as a bus parked on the side of Summit Avenue in the picture was blocking me from seeing anything beyond the street itself.

With a sigh, I heaved my bag up higher on my shoulder again and retraced my steps, studying the trees on the phone image and hoping to match the branches to anything around me.

"Mind the hostas," someone said to me, and I nearly jumped out of my skin.

"Excuse me?" I said, trying to find the woman to go with the voice.

"The hostas," she said again, and I spotted her. Her yard was completely enclosed by a dense hedge that she could just barely look over. Her face was deeply wrinkled, and a shock of chaotically frizzy gray hair jutted out from under her sunhat, as if refusing to be tamed. Her dark brown eyes darted down to the ground, then back up at my face, like she was using them to point at something.

I looked down. There at my feet was a row of small hostas. I had veered a bit to one side while looking at my phone and nearly had stepped off the sidewalk I had been so anxious not to block the middle of, although surely not so far as to disturb her plantings. Still, I felt the need to apologize.

"I'm very sorry. I shouldn't walk distracted," I said.

"It's just that they're new," the woman said. "Challenge enough to keep them going, what with all the dog traffic."

"Yes, I suppose," I said. "I wonder if you can help me? I'm looking for a house that should be here between yours and that condo building, but I don't see it."

The woman's eyes narrowed in suspicion. "That's not kind," she said.

"Pardon me?" I asked.

"I know I'm old, but my mind is as sharp as ever," she went on.

"I'm sure that's true," I said, confused.

"As are my eyes," she continued.

"Okay," I said, not sure what I had done to offend her. "Sorry," I said again.

"You should be," she said, still determined to be annoyed with me. "It's not like anyone could miss it."

"Well, I'm afraid I have," I said, and her eyes narrowed still further. There was no getting out of hot water with this woman, apparently. I looked down at the phone in my hand and realized at once how I could win her over. "Perhaps I missed it because I was looking at my phone."

"Those things are a nuisance," she said with a certain gleeful vitriol. "You nearly trod on my hostas looking at your phone."

"I *am* sorry," I said. "But I was using it to help me find the house. Only the picture on my phone is just a bus, and I can't even see..."

I trailed off as I glanced behind me, mid-gesture to show the woman where I had been when I had started looking at my phone.

There, towering over me, was a Queen Anne house complete with tower topped with a spire, covered front porch that made the front door appear to be in the back of a cavern, elaborate carvings in the details around the windows and along the rooftop. The sort of place the Addams Family would buy if they wanted to up size.

How had I missed it? I was standing in its shadow. The breeze felt chilly out of the sun, now that I was noticing it. How had I walked right past it not once, but twice?

In my defense, it was a very narrow house. I couldn't see how far back it extended, not past the trees that grew crowding close around it, but if the width was anything to judge by this had to be the smallest house I'd seen since walking up the street from the bus stop.

"There it is," I said wonderingly.

"That's what you're looking for?" the woman asked. I had upset her again.

"Yes," I said, my eyes finding the house number over the doorbell. The brass numerals were a dark green, all but blending into the brick.

"Your parties are too loud," the woman said.

"My parties?" I asked.

"Every weekend, more parties," she groused. "Every night in the summertime. It's ridiculous."

I sensed a trap. If I pointed out I had just arrived and didn't, in fact, live here, would she accuse me of ageism again?

"I'm sorry about that," I said. "But really, I'm only here for the weekend. But while I am here, I promise, I'll tell everyone to keep it down."

"Tell who?" the woman asked, eyes narrowing again as she quizzed me.

"Um," I said. "Cynthia Thomas?"

"She's rarely here," the woman said. "She ought to be here more. Keep a firmer hand on things. That man she hired to watch the place is far too permissive. Too many parties," she said, stressing each word.

"I'll let her know," I promised.

"If she's even here," the woman said.

"If she isn't, she will be soon," I said. "I'm meeting her specifically."

For some reason, she still didn't seem to believe me. I wondered who had lied to her, and how pervasively, to make her so untrusting.

"Mrs. Olson, I do hope you aren't scaring off new neighbors," someone said. I looked up to see a man walking towards me, the man who had just jogged past with the dog.

He was talking to the old woman, but those green eyes were fixed just on me, and for the first time in a very long time I remembered that sometimes I got intense, not to be ignored feelings that were of a very different nature from my not-quite-precognition.

I didn't know anything about this guy, not even his name, but as he drew to a stop towering over me, smiling down at me with those eyes like darkest jade, I wanted to know everything. And I wanted him to tell it to me slowly, over a lifetime.

I mean, on some level, I knew this wasn't any more rational than those other feelings. But it wasn't the level I was currently operating on, if you know what I mean.

CHAPTER 3

Only the powers that be know how long I stood there like that. Just gaping up at him. If I had been a computer, I'd have been one that needed its mouse jiggled to wake it back up.

But he didn't seem to notice either. The earbuds were hanging around his neck now, and he had pulled a hoodie on over the T-shirt he had been running in, but he clearly hadn't showered yet. His dark blond hair was drying in sweaty clumps that stuck out at all angles, but mostly straight up.

Messy as that hairstyle was at the moment, I felt a pang of familiarity. It was like all the boys back home had after they came home from the army, a soldier's cut that was just starting to grow out. Not long enough to comb flat, but too long to really be a buzz cut anymore.

"She's not a neighbor," the woman said, breaking the silence. Which was just as well; we couldn't stand there forever, no matter how much I kind of wanted to.

I noticed the edge had gone out of her voice. Whoever this man was, the old woman was at least grudgingly fond of him.

"No, I'm not," I confirmed. "I'm just here for the weekend."

"Ah," he said, nodding and glancing back at the Queen Anne house.

I doubted he had ever missed seeing it. "Well, even if just for the weekend, welcome to the neighborhood. I'm Nick Larson," he said, wiping his hand on his track pants before extending it to me. That must have done the trick; his hand in mine was warm but not sticky or slimy in the least.

"Amanda Clarke," I said. "Pleased to meet you."

"She's not from around here," the woman said. "Her manners are too good."

I felt my cheeks coloring. The corner of Nick's mouth lifted ever so slightly, and I knew he saw me turning pink, which promptly made me turn vividly red.

"Since she knows all about manners, I'm sure Ms. Olson has already introduced herself," he said.

"Mrs.," the woman swiftly corrected him.

"Of course," Nick said. "But is that Mrs. Frank Olson, or Mrs. Linda Olson? I can never remember which is correct."

Her mouth twisted as she fought the urge to smile at his gentle teasing. Once she had it under control, she said, "Mrs. Olson will be fine. I'm going in now; it's time for my show." She started to turn away, but quickly looked back at me. "Mind the hostas."

I looked down at the toes of my high-top sneakers, still nowhere near her plants. When I looked up again, she was gone.

"She's interesting," I said. Nick looked at me closely, and I felt myself blushing again.

"Interesting," he said, but he wasn't repeating my assessment. He was making one of his own, about me.

"What?" I asked.

"You really mean that," he said. "I'm sure she harassed you from the minute she started speaking to you, but you don't call her an angry old bat or anything. And I can tell by looking at you that you really mean it."

"I don't think you can," I said, fighting the urge to cover my cheeks. "You don't know that."

"You weren't just being nice," he insisted. "You really didn't notice she was a complete shrew."

"Honestly!" I said. "I would never call someone I just met something like that."

Nick grinned. "In this case, it wouldn't be apt anyway," he said. "Linda has arthritis. Her whole body hurts her all the time, and it can make her terse or grumpy. But when she's feeling well, she's a treasure. Funny and charming, and she knows everything about the neighborhood. But you had no way of knowing that. This isn't one of her good days. You're just... kind."

"Oh, I...," I wanted to contradict him, but I couldn't put the words together. Didn't everyone try to be kind? Wasn't that the whole point of being around other people?

"So you're just here for the weekend," he said.

"Yes," I said. "I'm here to see Cynthia Thomas. Do you know her?"

"Maybe by sight, but not by name," Nick said. "I don't actually live here either. My grandfather has a condo in the building next door. He's not been feeling well this week, so I've been coming over to walk his dog, Finnegan, and help out with the housework."

"And yet you know Linda?" I said.

"Linda," Nick said with a conspiratorial grin, "makes sure she knows everyone. As you've just seen firsthand."

I smiled. She had indeed made sure I had noticed she was there, all but hidden behind her hedge.

"Well, if you're here all weekend, perhaps I'll see you again," he said, taking a few steps backward, toward a compact car parked in front of the condo building.

"I hope so," I said. "It was good meeting you."

That grin spread across his tanned face once more. "There's that sincerity again." Then he turned, opening the car doors with a double beep, and then he was gone.

I looked up at the building that was still looming over me, not exactly welcoming me in.

Well, at least it hadn't disappeared again.

I put my phone away, then climbed the worn steps up to the porch. The air was even chillier here, as if the sun never touched this place.

I had seen the house numbers from the street, faded though they had been by oxidization of the brass and what looked like decades-old soot from coal fires clinging to the brick.

What I had missed entirely was a smaller brass plaque just over the cracked doorbell button. I leaned down, then pulled the sleeve of my sweater down over my hand to rub at the plaque.

Briefly, the letters seemed to glow brighter, like the flaming letters on the ring in that Hobbit movie, before fading back to obscurity. I had just had time to read all the words before they were gone.

MISS ZENOBIA WEEKES' CHARM SCHOOL FOR EXCEPTIONAL YOUNG LADIES.

Not for the first time, I had a feeling of unease, like a ghost passing through me. Why was I here, really? Why me? No one looked at me and thought "charm school."

I hadn't extended a finger to press the doorbell or raised a hand to grasp the heavy knocker ring that hung on the center of the door. I might even have been thinking seriously of walking back down those steps and all the way back home.

But the door opened with an anguished groan, and there was Cynthia Thomas in a silver cashmere sweater I was sure cost more than I made in a year over shiny black trousers. A beautiful silver locket hung from her neck, as quietly elegant as the rest of her.

"Ah, Amanda Clarke," she said with a smile. "So good to see you again. Please, step inside. And welcome to Charm School."

As I stepped through the doorway into the front hall, I felt a little shiver dance over the back of my neck. It wasn't a chill; it was warmer inside the house than on the sunless porch. It was something else. Something that made all the little hairs at the nape of my neck rise up at once. The swing of my ponytail tickled my suddenly sensitive skin.

"Everything all right?" Cynthia asked me with a little frown.

"Yes, I'm fine," I said, rubbing at the back of my neck until the shivery feeling went away. Cynthia continued to look at me intently, the little furrow between her eyebrows deepening. "Really, I'm fine," I said again. "When you said this place was a school, this really wasn't what I was expecting."

"I suppose calling it a school is more by way of an honorific,"

Cynthia said, indicating I should go through an open set of French doors to a sunny room to the left. "The girls who were her students attended other schools for academics. Miss Zenobia just guided us in the final polish, as it were."

"Oh, you were a student?" I said.

"Once upon a time," Cynthia said with a soft smile. The room we were standing in was what I believed you called a parlor: chairs, a love seat, and a sofa huddled close around a fireplace. Ideal for cozy conversation, with no television in sight anywhere.

"If you were a student, why am I here?" I asked. "I know you said she had no family, but surely you, being an actual student, trumps me being a former student's daughter. Why aren't you Miss Zenobia's successor or whatever?"

"That's complicated," Cynthia said, folding her hands together and summoning another smile. "I really don't want to go too deeply into it. The others haven't yet arrived, and they will doubtless have questions as well. No, I'd prefer to take all of your inquiries at once, after the reading of the will. It will make more sense then, I promise you."

"Okay," I agreed, twisting the handles of my bag in my hands. I was afraid to sit on any of the furniture. It was all in excellent condition, the wood gleaming from a recent polishing, the bright sapphire color of the upholstery not the least faded despite the sunbeams criss-crossing over them. But they were all clearly old. Old and expensive.

Somewhere further in the depths of the house, a door opened, then closed. Cynthia lifted a finger to beg my indulgence, then poked her head back out into the hall.

"I say, Mr. Trevor? I wonder if I might detain you for a moment?"

"Always at your disposal, Mrs. Thomas," a warm male voice answered. A gray-haired man appeared in the doorway. He was dressed in dark slacks, button-up shirt with the sleeves rolled up past the elbows, and sweater vest that appeared to be hand knit. It was pretty far from any sort of uniform, but something about his posture in the doorway screamed "butler."

"Mr. Trevor," Cynthia said, "May I present Miss Amanda Clarke."

"Miss Amanda," he said, taking my hand in both of his and clasping it tightly as he shook it. He looked me over again and again. "You look just like her. It's uncanny."

"You knew my mother?" I guessed.

"Only from photos, but I know Miss Zenobia had a special place in her heart for your mother," he said, and a sadness passed over his face. "A tale for another time, perhaps," he said with a glance at Cynthia.

"It will be easier to tell such stories when everyone has gathered," she said.

"How many others are coming?" I asked.

"Only two," Cynthia said. "You three are the only remaining descendants of the last class."

"Really?" I asked.

"Miss Zenobia took fewer and fewer students near the end," Mr. Trevor said.

"Less call for charm in these modern times," Cynthia said. I sensed she was diverting me from asking more questions. Indeed, I had a million of them, not the least being what Mr. Trevor meant by "near the end." My mother would have been a student more than twenty-five years ago, and Miss Zenobia had died only the month before. How old had she been?

Mr. Trevor seemed to notice the bag in my hand for the first time. "Shall I show Miss Amanda to her room?" he asked.

"Yes, lovely," Cynthia said. "Do give her the full tour. With all appropriate warnings," she added.

"Warnings?" I asked. "What sort of warnings?" I supposed a building as old as the one I was standing in presented all sorts of hazards, fussy heating elements with the potential to cause fires or tricky electrical switches or something.

At least, that's what I told myself would need a warning. The less logical part of my brain was convinced the building was haunted, and the warnings would be which hallways never to go down after dark, or locked rooms better left undisturbed.

That shiver started to ripple up the back of my neck again. I was a bit too exuberant clapping a hand over it this time. The loud slap echoed through the parlor, and both Mr. Trevor and Cynthia gave me quizzical looks.

"Mosquito?" I offered.

"A little late in the year for those," Cynthia said. "We had a frost a few nights ago."

"We did, they didn't," Mr. Trevor murmured, then added more loudly, "And some of the screens do need mending. Come, Miss Amanda. You've seen the parlor. Allow me to show you the rest of the school."

"That would be lovely," I said, hoisting my bag back over my shoulder, but carefully. Every table and shelf and fireplace mantle around me was covered in an array of small, breakable objects, any one of which was surely worth more than I made in a month, even with tips.

I would have to keep the flailing to a minimum if I felt that chill running up my spine again.

CHAPTER 4

Mr. Trevor led me down the central hallway towards the back of the house. "Through there is what they call the butler's pantry," he said, pointing into a long, narrow space filled with cupboards and countertops covered with such things as a complete tea service in gleaming silver, large china platters, and domes to put over plates like people in movies have with their hotel room service. "The extra linen is in there as well, should the need arise," he added.

"Okay," I said, not sure what I would need linen for, especially as I was only staying for the weekend.

"Over here is the dining room," he said, pointing to the room on the left side of the hall. The table that dominated the space was massive. It looked like it had been carved from one immense block of solid wood with scraps left over large enough to craft the tall-backed chairs that crowded around it.

I wondered what kind of tree was so large and had wood so dark. It seemed to pull the light out of the air, consuming it voraciously.

The far side of the room was bowed out into the side garden, three separate windows surrounding a padded seat. Ever since I was a kid, I had wanted to curl up in a window seat with a good, long book, but this spot was too dark to look at all inviting.

Perhaps later in the day, the effect would be less severe.

The largest chair was at the head of the table, closest to the hall and directly facing the bay window. Sitting on the table before the chair was a box fashioned from an even darker wood, with brass fastenings that gleamed dully. Something about the box called out to me, and my steps slowed. As Mr. Trevor continued down the hall with a prattle of words, I paid no attention to I found myself standing beside that chair.

What was in that box? It was rather low and flat, and I suspected it contained flatware, perhaps silver like the tea service in the pantry. Or maybe it was a particularly fancy tea chest.

"Please don't touch that, Miss Amanda," Mr. Trevor said. I blinked, and it was like being suddenly awake after dozing off on a hot summer day. I couldn't have been out of it for more than a second or two, just long enough for Mr. Trevor to notice I had lagged behind and to come back for me.

"I wasn't going to open it," I said, wincing inside at the sullen sound of my own voice. What was wrong with me?

"I'm sure you weren't," Mr. Trevor said gently, but then I felt his hand close over mine and realized I had been grasping the front clasp. I had half-lifted that little bronze latch already.

"Oh," I said, snatching my hand back and cradling it close to my chest as if the box had burned me. "I'm so sorry."

"Please don't worry about it," Mr. Trevor said. "I hadn't expected this to be sitting out, or I would have warned you."

"Warned me?" I repeated.

"For the time being, until you have your feet under you, it would be wisest not to touch the things," he said.

"Which things?" I asked.

"To be on the safe side, anything," he said. "But certainly not any of the boxes or flasks or other containers. None of them are empty."

His eyebrows arched up as he said that, as if it were a code, and I should be inferring some meaning from his words, but I had no clue what it could mean that nothing was empty.

But not touching anything was a rule I could follow, so I just nodded.

He picked up the box and set it on the very top of the hutch that stood against the back wall. Then he turned back to me with a smile.

"Let's continue on to the kitchen," he said, this time guiding me to precede him down the hall to the next sunny room on the right. The cabinets and even the table and chairs looked like they had stood there for decades, but the appliances were new. "I've stocked up for the weekend, lots of snacks and beverages to see you through between meals. Please feel free to help yourself to anything, and if there is anything you need, just let me know. I always end up doing a bit of shopping when I'm on my morning walk, so it's really no trouble."

"Thank you," I said, ignoring the sudden growling of my stomach at the mention of food. I didn't want to interrupt the tour, especially as I had inadvertently done so once already.

The kitchen had two doors that opened onto the central hallway. Having gone in one, Mr. Trevor led the way out the other. Directly across from that doorway was a steep, narrow staircase. Mr. Trevor opened the door on his left, the door that stood at the very end of the hallway. The door itself was largely frosted glass, letting in light but too opaque to see details through.

"This is the solarium," Mr. Trevor said, stepping into the room beyond. It was like being inside a greenhouse with plants on tiered shelves on the three glassed walls, a small cast iron table and chairs sitting against the brick wall that divided this space from the kitchen itself. "Miss Zenobia always took her morning tea here. She loved the smell of her plants and the warmth of the morning sun. It's too late in the day now, but perhaps tomorrow you will see what I mean."

"I'll be sure to check it out," I promised.

"This door leads to the back porch," he said, opening a clear glass door to show me a narrow porch that ended in a short flight of steps that led to a series of stepping stones. Some of the stepping stones led further back through the raised garden beds to a small orchard at the back garden wall. Others curved around the corner of the house to the side garden of flowering plants that clustered around the dining room bay window.

"It's all so lovely," I said. "Even for late September. So much is still blooming, and those dark red blossoms are fascinating."

"I choose the plantings carefully," Mr. Trevor said, and he couldn't hide the pride in his smile, although I sensed he was generally a rather humble person. "I like to have something in bloom from the earliest of spring to the latest of autumn."

"I'll have to take a walk around if I have the time," I said.

"We'll take the main stairs up to the second floor," Mr. Trevor said, leading me back down the hall past the dining room to the stairs I had passed without noticing when I had come out of the parlor. These stairs were not so steep as the back stairs, only going up five steps at a time before reaching a landing and making a turn. Three turns to go up one level, and I could see at least two more levels above, although the light fixture that hung down from the top of the house dazzled my eyes when I tried to look up to the top floor.

"The library and Miss Zenobia's office are on this level," Mr. Trevor said as we stepped off the staircase. The low roof over the front porch made sense now as I looked out on the high-walled porch that stood over it. Small trees in massive urns stood at regular intervals around the curve of the porch, and a few more cast-iron chairs were scattered around.

Then we were in the library, and my breath caught. My hometown had a public library, and I had spent many endless hours there as a kid, enjoying the one thing I didn't need any pocket change to get access to. I had thought so many times about how that little building contained more than I could ever hope to read in a thousand years.

Miss Zenobia's library was three times as large. Shelves ran from the floor to the ceiling high above, row after row of shelves. At the center of the room was another table of heavy, dark wood, narrower but longer than the dining room table. Chairs were drawn up neatly all around it, and four of those places had their own little lights, the brass kind with green glass that directed the light straight down for optimal reading.

"I didn't know charm schools had so much reading," I said, resisting the temptation to run my fingers along the spines. Books could contain things the same as boxes or flasks.

"Miss Zenobia's school was quite singular," Mr. Trevor said. The light in the library was dim, but I could swear his cheeks were flushing. He cleared his throat and looked around for some distraction. "Ah, yes. There are many artifacts in this room, on the shelves and in the storage spaces under the window seats. Best not to touch any of them, for now."

"All right," I agreed. It occurred to me that was the second time he had implied I would be touching things later.

When I got my feet under me. What did that mean?

"The rooms at the end of the hall are mine," he said, indicating the closed door with a wave of his hand. "And this is Miss Zenobia's office. Best to avoid that as well."

I peeked into the room as we walked back towards the stairs. Her office was directly over the dining room. Behind the desk and chair was another matching bay window. I could see the branches of a tree close enough to scratch at the glass if there had been a breeze.

The room was stuffed full with objects. Something that looked like a cauldron was sitting before a fireplace. It appeared to be full of gemstones and crystals. The mantel was cluttered with little brass machines like antique versions of office toys.

A carpet was rolled up and leaning in one corner. What was that all about?

Mr. Trevor, standing with one foot on the staircase up, cleared his throat and I hurried to his side.

"There is one more level, but that's just the attic space."

"Full of things not to be touched?" I guessed.

"Right in one," he said with a grin. "Miss Zenobia's room is here on the left, overlooking the front lawn. No need to go in there."

"Of course," I agreed.

"This here is the bathroom. I'm afraid there's just the one. It is a very old house," he said.

"I'm sure it will be fine," I said as we walked past a room on the left done all in green and gold, and another on the right done in cream and rose with a bay window. The tree was even fuller at this height, thick branches seeming to hug the side of the house.

"I've put you in here if that's all right," he said, opening the door at the very end of the hall. "It overlooks the back garden."

"Lovely," I said, barely more than a whisper.

Or perhaps it was the immensity of the space swallowing up my voice. My entire apartment back home wasn't as big as this room. The bedspread, carpet, and wallpaper were all blue and silver, and the furniture was carved from some type of honey-colored wood.

"It's really lovely," I said again.

"I'll leave you to settle in then," Mr. Trevor said. "I ring the bell for dinner at precisely 6:30. Oh, and the Wi-Fi password is on the card on the nightstand."

"Thank you so much," I said.

Mr. Trevor gave me one last welcoming smile, then hastened to join Cynthia downstairs. I looked around the room at the antique furniture; the elaborate rug spread out before the fireplace, the lushly thick bedspread.

Even the little bench at the foot of the bed looked like something that should be in a museum. Far too fine of a piece of furniture for the likes of my bag. The bag I had used through every year of high school to carry my books, now repurposed to be my one piece of luggage on the only trip I'd taken out of my hometown since high school.

I didn't fit in here at all.

But there was hope yet. I didn't know a thing about the others that Cynthia had summoned to also attend the reading of the will, but surely at least one of them would feel as out of place as I did.

A little bell at the end of the hall started ringing. Was that the doorbell?

Forgetting both my hunger and my need for a nap, I left my bag there on the hardwood floor and went back to the top of the stairs.

I had to get a look at who was at the door now.

CHAPTER 5

The third floor landing was level with the top of the light fixture, making looking down to the first floor and expecting to see anything a questionable proposition.

I glanced up at where the chain and electrical cable were anchored at the highest point of the sloped ceiling another level above me and felt a momentary stab of curiosity. What had Mr. Trevor failed to show me? Was he hiding something up there?

But then I heard Cynthia Thomas downstairs swinging the heavy door open and calling out a cheery hello, and that same curiosity stabbed me again, this time poking me until I started creeping down the stairs to where I could get a better look.

Honestly, it was like my curiosity was a pirate sometimes, pushing me out on precarious planks over shark-filled waters with constant pokes from the end of a sword. Someday it would likely get me killed.

But not today. Today, it just wanted me to get a better look at the other girls who had been summoned to Miss Zenobia's Charm School for Exceptional Young Ladies. Did the "exceptional" label fit them better than it did me?

"Did you find the house all right, Miss Brianna?" Cynthia was asking.

"Um, yes," a young woman said distractedly. I still couldn't see her. I crept down a few more steps. This was just the sort of house that would have a trick step, one that would squeak loudly and give me away. At least my shoes were silent. I had been wearing the same pair of Converse high-tops since my senior year of high school, and the soles were nearly paper thin, but a ninja couldn't ask for anything stealthier.

"You look flustered," Cynthia said.

"Oh," Brianna answered, as if she hadn't realized her own emotional state. "There was a woman next door..."

"Say no more," Cynthia said with a smile in her voice. "Mrs. Olson has that effect on everyone."

"Oh," Brianna said again. She sounded like someone constantly startled to find herself in the middle of a conversation.

I reached the landing at the second floor and was finally far enough below the light and at the correct angle to see the reception area in front of the door. But Cynthia was just leading the girl into the parlor. I only caught a glimpse of a girl about my age in black tights and ankle boots, a plaid skirt and burgundy button-up top that made her look like a hip librarian, especially when she looked back over her shoulder and I caught the glint from her cat-eye glasses. Very librarian.

I would have thought that burgundy would clash with the deeply red hair that hung in a sleek sheet to the middle of her back, but the two colors complemented each other, and felt very appropriate for the autumn that was just beginning to touch the trees outside.

"Miss Amanda," Mr. Trevor said, suddenly at my elbow. I just managed not to yelp in surprise. "I'm sure Mrs. Thomas would be delighted to introduce you to Miss Brianna Collins. Having you all meet ahead of time is why we asked you to arrive the day before the reading."

"Yes, of course," I said. "Do none of us know each other?"

"Not yet," he said with a smile, then brushed past me to lead the way down the stairs.

In the parlor, the monosyllabic Miss Brianna had somehow trans-formed into a monologuing motormouth. The flood of words pouring out of her were all but drowning Cynthia, who looked almost panicked but somehow managed to keep the polite smile on her lips, her hands clasped together in front of her as she nodded at every pause that slipped into Brianna's speech.

"It's crucial, you see. Crucial," she said. "I worked in a break to come here because you said it was so very important, but it can really only be the tiniest of breaks. I brought books with me, but not nearly enough, and I'm losing so much time."

She slipped the backpack off of her shoulders as she said this and set it on the ground at her feet. It landed with a deep thud. I doubted it contained anything but books, although there must be a toothbrush and a change of clothes in there somewhere.

She had walked up Summit Avenue with all that on her back? She looked so scrawny.

"Mrs. Thomas," Mr. Trevor said, and the look of relief that washed over Cynthia's face was pronounced.

"Ah, Mr. Trevor. And Miss Amanda! Excellent!" she said. "Miss Amanda, may I present Miss Brianna Collins? And Miss Brianna, this is Miss Amanda Clarke."

"Hello," I said. The little word sounded all wrong after all that formal speech.

"Pleased to meet you," Brianna said. I assume to me. Her eyes were focused somewhere in the vicinity of my feet.

"Brianna joins us from Boston, Massachusetts," Cynthia said and seemed to have more to say, but Brianna swiftly interrupted.

"I'm a student there," she said, still looking at various points around my feet. "I graduated last year with a double major in physics and library science. I'm getting a master's degree now, following a course of study of my own design. It's crucial I don't fall behind on my research. Very, very crucial."

"I imagine," I said, casting about for something more to say. "The school year just started, after all."

"Yes, precisely!" Brianna said, and for the quickest of seconds, she glanced up and looked me in the eye.

Then she was looking at the floor near Cynthia's feet. "I really shouldn't have come. I don't have the time, and it's such a distraction."

"I do realize," Cynthia said with deep sympathy. "You will see how important it is for you all to be here in person tomorrow night, I promise you."

Brianna nodded absentmindedly, but then another thought hit her like a bolt of lightning and her whole body tensed up. She looked directly at Cynthia, her eyes narrowing behind the cat-eye glasses.

"Did you compel me to come? Mental suggestion? Something in that tea?" she asked darkly.

"No, Miss Brianna!" Cynthia said, horrified. "I assure you, I don't have those sorts of skills. And I would never do such a thing!"

Brianna's eyes narrowed further, but then her full-body tension broke into a loose shrug.

"I suppose not," she said, and turned her attention to the room behind her.

Cynthia looked over at Mr. Trevor as if begging to be rescued.

"Mrs. Thomas, I wonder if I might pull you aside for a moment?" Mr. Trevor asked. "A small matter about dinner."

"Yes, of course," Cynthia said. "I'll just be a moment." She smiled at Brianna, who didn't seem to have heard any of that, then at me. Then she and Mr. Thomas disappeared down the hall.

What were they canoodling about? The oddness of Brianna Collins?

Brianna stepped up to the mantelpiece over the fireplace, gazing closely at each of the objects on display there. She reached out a delicate hand, barely grazing the surface of a sterling silver box lid with one fingertip, then, to my puzzlement, touching that fingertip to her tongue. Her eyebrows drew together as if she had a hard time placing the taste.

"This might be okay," she said. I wasn't sure if she was talking to me, herself, or the box.

"What do you mean?" I asked.

"There could be things to learn here," she said, and again I wasn't sure if she was speaking to me. It was a very odd feeling. If she kept it up, I just might start questioning whether I still even existed.

"It's strange here, isn't it?" she asked.

"It's an old house," I said.

"Not so very," she said with a dismissive shrug.

"No, I suppose in Boston there are houses which are much older," I said.

She shrugged again. "Parts of this house are older than others," she said and looked around the room. Nothing looked out of place to me, but I didn't know much about architecture or historical periods or anything like that. "It pulls to one side, kind of like. Doesn't it?" She tipped her head to one side, and I was certain she was asking the house itself this question, but then her eyes darted back to mine, that briefest of glances meeting before her gaze dropped away.

"I really don't know," I admitted, then found myself adding, "I didn't go to college myself. I work in a diner. So."

Brianna pursed her lips and almost scowled. "What *we* know doesn't come from *colleges*," she said, her voice practically dripping with disdain at that last word. "That's why I design my own course of study. None of the teachers are ever going to willingly teach me the good stuff."

"What's the good stuff?" I asked.

"You know," she said with a dismissive wave and turned her attention to a leather-bound book standing open on one of the end tables next to the sofa.

"I don't think I do," I said.

"This is interesting." She said under her breath as she turned the pages. She seemed to have completely lost the thread of the conversation, and I was delighted to let it drop.

"There's an entire library upstairs," I told her. "More books than we had in the public library in my hometown. Although I suppose the same wouldn't be true for you."

"A library? Here?" she asked, her green eyes dancing with excitement.

"Yes, a library," Mr. Trevor announced as he appeared in the doorway. "The highlight of the tour, but not where we begin. Shall I show you around?"

"Yes, please," Brianna said, bending over to pick up that massive bag. The thread that ran through the seams was stretched thin, tested to its very limits, but she got the weight of it back up onto her shoulders with barely a grunt.

She was stronger than she looked.

"Please, make yourself at home, Miss Amanda," Mr. Trevor said to me. "Remember, the kitchen is at your disposal, although do be sure not to spoil your dinner. Beef and sweet potato stew, loaded with herbs from Miss Zenobia's own plants. You'll want seconds, I'm sure."

"I'm looking forward to it," I said with a smile, putting a hand against my belly as if that could somehow quiet the loud growl that just naming the food out loud had provoked.

Alone in the parlor, I was still reluctant to sit on any of the furniture, but I did lean in to examine all the little items. I even closed my eyes and tried to sense the building itself all around me.

The library in my hometown was still my favorite place. I had a little TV with all the local channels in my apartment, but most evenings I curled up in my sofa bed and consumed novels. The library didn't get enough new stock for me to be too picky about what kinds of stories I read, but I always grabbed the new horror novels first. And I loved haunted house stories the best. I've read *The Haunting of Hill House* more than a dozen times and it still gives me the chills.

But try as I might, I couldn't feel anything odd about the building around me. Whatever Brianna was sensing, I didn't get the faintest hint of it.

But this time I didn't feel out of place. I doubted Mr. Trevor or Cynthia felt anything odd, either.

In fact, I bet Brianna had all sorts of perceptions that normal people didn't. She certainly seemed "exceptional," but not in a way that made me feel inferior.

Maybe we really were equals. She had feelings about the house. I sometimes woke up with feelings like compulsions that dictated my behavior. I just might belong here after all.

But the feeling of relief that washed over me turned cold as the doorbell rang again.

The last of us had arrived. And somehow the way she had rung the bell just sounded more authoritative than when I or Brianna had done it. What was this new girl going to be like?

CHAPTER 6

I lingered in the parlor as Cynthia once more wrestled the
heavy door open.

"Ah, Miss Sophie DuBois," Cynthia said.

"So this is the right place," Sophie said. She sounded almost disappointed. What had she been expecting? Certainly not something
bigger. "Can you hold the door open? I'll have the driver bring in my
bags."

Bags? Was she expecting to stay longer than Brianna and I were?

I heard the sounds of a winded man struggling up the front steps,
dropping something heavy, then shuffling back down to do it again
twice more.

"Thank you so much," Sophie said. I couldn't place her accent. It
sounded like she had been born in the south but moved to New York
or something. Definitely a city dweller, though. Even as she thanked
the driver, there was something a little... well, pushy in her tone.

"We'll leave your bags there for now," Cynthia said, and she
appeared in the doorway. She gave me a smile as she joined me near
the fireplace. "Oh good, you're still here. I can introduce you to Miss
Sophie DuBois. Miss Sophie, this is Miss Amanda Clarke."

I couldn't see Sophie's face as she came into the room. Her head was tipped down and the wide brim of her hat covered her features. I could tell by her bare arms that she was black, and that she kept herself in amazing shape.

I'm not so bad myself. I started lifting weights in high school as part of my hockey training and I'd kept up with it. Mostly. But Sophie was leaner than I could ever hope to be.

She tipped her head to take her hat off with a flourish, running a hand through the patch of curls that rested on her forehead. The back and sides of her head were cut close, and she soon had the longer tangle of curls in the front standing prettily.

My own hair wasn't so kind when I wore hats.

"Pleased to meet you," I said, holding out my hand. Sophie was about my height but nearly half my size. But not in a scrawny way. From the way she moved as she stepped forward to take my hand, I was certain she was a dancer or a gymnast.

"Charmed," Sophie said, looking me over. Her gaze swept past my shapeless sweater and worn jeans to linger on my beloved sneakers.

I didn't get the sense she approved. She was wearing sneakers as well, but the sort that cost a lot more than I would ever spend on shoes. They glowed up at me, flawlessly white, and I was pretty sure she had ironed her jeans.

"Mrs. Thomas? A moment?" Mr. Trevor asked from the doorway.

"Of course, please excuse me," Cynthia said with a smile for each of us.

I was starting to think these little conferences in the other room were a ruse, like they really just wanted to leave us alone together for a moment. What were they expecting to happen? Bonding?

Somehow, I thought I stood even less of a chance of bonding with Sophie than I had with Brianna. Still, I had to give it a try.

"It's lovely, isn't it?" I said, then waved a hand at the room around us when her puzzled frown told me she had no idea what I was referring to.

"Is it?" she asked, looking around. "I suppose it's about what I expected." She wrinkled her nose ever so slightly.

"You don't like it?" I asked.

Sophie tipped her head to one side and scrunched up her face.

"I prefer more modern architecture," she said.

"Like the condos next door," I said.

"Exactly," she said. "I would love to see inside that building."

"I met someone who lives there. Well, his grandfather does," I amended. "If I run into him again, I can ask if he'll show us inside."

Sophie gave me an assessing look, but she seemed to be distracted by the sudden arrival of Brianna before she could come to any conclusions about me.

"Sophie, this is Brianna," I said as Brianna ground to a halt in the doorway, almost as if she had expected the parlor to be empty.

"Hello," Brianna said, once more looking at the floor.

"Hey yourself," Sophie said in a lazy drawl.

"Brianna is from Boston," I said, and Brianna nodded vigorously. "I'm from northern Iowa. Dairy farm country. I can't place your accent?"

"My accent is Creole," Sophie said, and I could tell she was telling me that with all the extra Creole she could muster. "I'm from New Orleans, born and bred."

"Ooh, I've always wanted to go there," Brianna said, so excited she almost looked directly at Sophie. "So much history."

"Indeed," Sophie said. "I never want to live anywhere else." She looked around the room again, still disapproving.

"Doesn't New Orleans also have a lot of old homes?" I asked.

"I don't mind old things," Sophie said, her tone almost chastising. "I just prefer new. Old things come with so much baggage."

I had the nearly overwhelming urge to point out that Sophie herself had arrived with quite a lot of baggage for a weekend stay, but I managed to bite my tongue just in the nick of time.

"I know what you mean," Brianna said, lowering her voice nearly to a whisper. "This place feels older than it is."

I expected Sophie to laugh that off, but she didn't. She bit at her lip and got a faraway look in her eyes.

"Parts of it are older than others," I said. "That's what you said before, right, Brianna?"

Brianna didn't seem to hear me, but Sophie said, "yes."

"It pulls to one side," Brianna said, not quite meeting Sophie's eyes.

"It does," Sophie said, sounding as if she were surprised to find that to be true.

"What does that mean?" I asked. "How does a house pull?"

"Don't you feel it?" Sophie asked.

"Feel what?" I closed my eyes and tried to sense... anything. But there was nothing. "What are you feeling? Like the house slopes to one side? Like it's settling more on one side than the other?"

I opened my eyes to find them both staring at me like they thought I was trying to pull a prank on them.

Like I was lying. Just pretending not to know what they meant.

"No," Sophie said. "That's not what we mean."

She looked like she wanted to say more, but Cynthia was back in the parlor with Mr. Trevor in tow.

"Miss Sophie, this is Mr. Trevor," Cynthia said, and Sophie gave me one last backward glance before crossing the room to shake his hand.

"I see you have a lot of luggage," Mr. Trevor said.

"I'm between gigs," Sophie said. "They wouldn't hold my place," she added to Cynthia. Her face remained impassive, but I was certain that Sophie was fighting to hide a huge amount of disappointment about something mixed with a certain amount of resentment directed at Cynthia.

"I *am* sorry," Cynthia said, clutching her hands together. "You'll understand tomorrow night why we really couldn't move the date."

Sophie nodded. I didn't think she was so much agreeing with Cynthia as that she didn't trust herself to speak in that moment.

"Shall we?" Mr. Trevor said.

"Certainly," Sophie said, picking up her hat from where she had set it on the back of one of the chairs.

"I can help bring some of the bags upstairs," I offered. "Which room?"

"The room on the right side of the hall," Mr. Trevor told me. "Do leave the heavier bags for me."

"No need," I said. "I'm stronger than I look."

I felt a touch on my arm and looked over to see Brianna standing beside me, giving my biceps a probing squeeze. "You look plenty strong," she said.

"Thanks?" I said. "I used to play hockey on a team full of farm girls. Now they were seriously strong."

Sophie gave a soft laugh, but I could see by her eyes that she was genuinely amused by my comment and not mocking me. I smiled back.

"I'll help too," Brianna said. "Just the light bags for me, though."

"Remember, dinner at 6:30," Mr. Trevor told us as I picked up two of the bags, then promptly handed the lighter of the two to Brianna and reached for something heavier.

"Just enough time to freshen up," Cynthia said.

"Do we dress for dinner?" Brianna asked, as if she wasn't already in a skirt. "I mean, it is a charm school. That feels like a dress for dinner kind of place."

"It's not necessary," Cynthia said to my enormous relief. My bag upstairs might have cleaner clothes than what I had been wearing for the last thirty hours across two states by bus, but it didn't have anything fancier.

It took Brianna and me three trips to get all the bags up to Sophie's room on the third floor. We made a mountain of luggage at the foot of her bed, then went back out into the hallway.

"I'm in here," Brianna said, pointing across the hall.

"I'm at the end, there," I said.

"Cool." She glanced from the toes of her own shoes over to the toes of mine. "See you at dinner."

"See you," I said. "I wanted to take a shower. Do you need the bathroom?"

"No, go ahead," she said, then disappeared into her room.

The moment I was back in my room, I regretted skipping the opportunity for a nap. But surely no one would mind if I went straight to bed after dinner. The important events weren't until the next night, anyway.

I found towels in the armoire, but also a lush bathrobe of a deep royal blue that matched the rest of the room. I undressed, slipped into the robe, and, hugging a towel to my chest, headed down the hall to the bathroom.

I turned on the shower, then closed my eyes as I waited for the water to get warm.

Try as I might, I couldn't sense anything about the house around me. It just felt like a house.

It was one thing for someone odd like Brianna to talk about sensing things, but Sophie seemed like someone who always approached things rationally, with cold logic. And yet she talked about sensing things too. Were they messing with me, or did they really have some kind of extrasensory perception?

What did the exceptional in Exceptional Young Ladies mean, exactly?

I gave myself a shake, then took off the robe and got into the warmth of the shower. I was being silly. The charm school had been around in the early days of the twentieth century, right? Clearly "exceptional" was nothing more than code for "rich."

Which meant that I definitely wasn't the kind of exceptional they were looking for.

So why was I here?

Somehow, I knew if I asked, I'd just be told that it would all make sense tomorrow.

I wished it were tomorrow already.

CHAPTER 7

I lingered too long under that deliciously hot water, fogging up not just the mirror but the entire bathroom. I would have expected a house so old would offer the same showers I was used to in my apartment back home: lukewarm with very little water pressure. The moment I stepped under that blast of water it was like a full body massage, finding all the little aches and pains from my long day on the bus and spiriting them away.

I don't remember getting out of the shower. I do remember wrapping the robe back around myself, thick and fluffy like a blanket.

The hardwood floor in the hallway and bedroom was cold under my bare feet and I raced to the bed to stand on the rug while I dug out clean clothes.

At least, that had been the plan. But the zipper on my bag was stuck, and I sat down on the bed to get a closer look at it.

Then—and this I don't remember at all, but I must have done it—I laid down and drifted off to sleep.

It wasn't a really deep sleep. I kind of felt like I was still awake, but in too blissful a state to bother with moving.

I thought I heard a radio playing in some other part of the house, some trick of acoustics bringing the tinny sound to my ears. As I drifted closer to slumber, the music would grow louder, then dimming again when I rousted almost to the point of opening my eyes.

It felt like this went on forever, but the spell was broken by a hand on my shoulder, roughly shaking me.

"Wha...?" I stammered, clutching the robe around me as I hiked up on one elbow.

"You fell asleep," Brianna said, stepping back as if touching me had burned her. "The others are waiting in the dining room. It's time to eat."

"Oh!" I said, rubbing at my face and looking around for a clock. I didn't see one. "I'm sorry. I'll be right down."

"I'll tell them," Brianna said and turned to head back out the door.

"Hey," I said, snapping fully awake. "Did you hear music just now?"

"Music?" she said with a frown.

"At first I thought someone in the house had a radio on, but just now it sounded more like a live band in the backyard," I said.

"I think you were dreaming," Brianna said. "You should get dressed now. Mr. Trevor is waiting for you before he dishes up the stew, and I don't think Sophie is the most patient person in the world."

"No, I don't think so either," I said. "I'll be right down."

But the moment she left the room, rather than reaching for my clothes, I hopped off the bed and looked out the window that over-looked the backyard. Nothing but plants and trees, and I wasn't hearing the music any longer.

But I really didn't think I had dreamed it. It must be some quirk of old house acoustics. Mr. Trevor looked like he could be a Cole Porter fan. Cynthia too, for that matter.

I shook out clothes that had gotten woefully wrinkled while packed together in my bag and pulled them on, then sat on the bed again to get my sneakers back on. I was about to go charging out of the room when I caught a glimpse of myself in the little mirror over the dresser.

I had laid down on the bed face-down, but not entirely. At some point, I had rolled my head to one side so I could breathe. And I could totally tell which side. Sleeping on wet hair was never a good idea. Now I had the mother of all cowlicks spinning over one temple, throwing my bangs in disarray and making one side of my thick, curly hair look oddly flat.

Brushing through it only made it worse. I dug a hairpin out of the front pouch of my bag and twisted the side up and back, then pinned it down over the cowlick. Not the most elegant of hairstyles, but it would have to be good enough.

If Sophie ever lightened up, I would have to ask her what her trick was for getting her own curls to obey her finger-combing even after being crushed by a hat. That sort of thing could really come in handy.

I thought I would save some time by running down the narrower back stairs, but I had to slow way down as the steps were narrower and steeper and, honestly, felt like they wanted to kill me.

I startled everyone by bursting into the dining room from the doorway opposite the one they were all watching. Sophie at least made an effort to pull the scowl from her face by pursing her lips and looking down in her own lap.

"Sorry," I said. "Unscheduled nap."

"We completely understand," Cynthia said, and Mr. Trevor murmured his agreement as he got to his feet and removed the cover from the tureen sitting in the center of the table to start filling bowls with steaming brown and orange stew. I started to slide into the closest empty seat but realized it was the one at the head of the table. There was no place setting in front of it, just the box still resting there as if waiting for something. I backed away from it and took the only other empty chair.

Why had Mr. Trevor taken that box back down?

Why did I still have the almost overwhelming urge to lift the lid?

What if I woke up in the morning and the "almost" dropped off that "overwhelming?" I had never fought that compulsive feeling before. But if I opened that box, what would happen?

I forced myself to shift my focus from the box to the other people around the table.

"Amanda had the longest journey," Cynthia was telling Brianna and Sophie.

"I thought she came from Iowa," Sophie said.

"I came by bus," I said. "I actually had to catch a ride into South Dakota first to get to the nearest bus station."

"That sounds terribly remote," Brianna said, giving a smile in the general direction of Mr. Trevor as he handed her a bowl of stew.

"I guess that's why they call it flyover country," Sophie said, not unkindly.

Mr. Trevor handed me my bowl last, and we all dug in. It was every bit as good as he had promised, and I wasn't just thinking that because I was so hungry and so sick of gas station sandwiches and prepackaged snacks.

We ate in companionable silence for a bit, but curiosity kept poking at my mind. Finally, I looked up at Cynthia and said, "I heard music, earlier. Cole Porter, I think? It sounded like it was coming from the backyard."

"I didn't hear it," Brianna reported between spoonfuls.

"Well, it is Friday night," Cynthia said, not quite looking at me. "It's a bit chilly for outdoor entertainment, but there are always a few hardy souls around here who will barbecue in a blizzard without batting an eye, so anything is possible."

"I think she dreamed it," Brianna persisted. "She was asleep when she heard it."

"A good night's sleep will do wonders," Cynthia said and smiled at me again before taking another bite of stew.

"I didn't sleep at all on the bus," I admitted. "Too many crank kids. Too many stops."

I really wasn't looking forward to the ride back. I doubted I would be well enough rested before it was time to go the day after tomorrow, especially as the reading of the will wouldn't start until midnight.

So many crazy stipulations. Miss Zenobia Weekes may have run a very fine school for exceptional young ladies back in her day, but she had also clearly been an eccentric.

"Are you going to see some of the town while you're here?" Sophie asked. "It's not New Orleans, but there must be museums and art galleries around here somewhere."

"And Minneapolis is just across the river," Brianna added.

"I suppose we have all day tomorrow since the reading isn't until midnight," I said. "But I really can't stay longer than Sunday. I don't get paid when I don't work, and a whole weekend off is more than I can afford, really."

"You have your bus ticket back already? Because my ticket was a one-way flight," Brianna said with a glance at Cynthia. "I thought it was a mistake?"

"Mine was too," Sophie said. "Hence the luggage. I didn't want to assume I was ever getting home again. Especially as I now don't have the position I earned in the premiere troupe I've spent my whole life working to get into."

"I can't be away either," Brianna said, as if she hadn't heard Sophie at all. "My research is at a crucial point. I'm so close to a breakthrough. I brought what I could carry, but already I've found that I left a text I absolutely need back home in Boston. I have to go home on Sunday as well."

"Whereas I can be here forever now," Sophie said, poking at the last bit of stew at the bottom of her bowl. "No reason to hurry back."

"I truly am sorry, all of you," Cynthia said. "I know coming here involved sacrifices on all of your parts, and that is made all the more meaningful because I could tell you so little about why you had to come."

"If we could just book my flight home? I like knowing what's going on. I like having a schedule. I have to be able to plan," Brianna said.

"Just one more day," Cynthia said. "Everything will make sense after the reading."

"You keep saying that," Sophie said.

"I know," Cynthia sighed and rubbed at her forehead. "It is the one truth I can share with you. But think about it, you know some things require delicate timing. If you think it through, weigh your feelings and what you sense through your intuition, I think you'll come to the conclusion that you can have just a little faith, and wait one more day."

Brianna glanced over at Sophie, who had a dreamy look on her face, as if she truly were going within to consult her intuition.

I was pretty sure my rare strong feelings weren't the sort of intuition that Cynthia was talking about. And anyway, I couldn't just consult with them on command.

"One day," Brianna said. I wasn't sure if she was agreeing to the terms or just merely restating them.

"I know it's asking a lot," Cynthia said. "But you three are special. Miss Zenobia tasked me with tracking you three down in particular. She taught many students over her long years, and those students have had countless children, grandchildren, and great-grandchildren. But it was you three she wanted summoned for the reading of her will."

"But I never even met her," I said.

"Me neither," Brianna said.

"I never even heard of her," Sophie said forcefully. "And if she's who you're implying she is, I really should have."

Cynthia bit her lip, and I could tell she was struggling with what she could say. She was a lawyer. She navigated rules I couldn't even contemplate, I was sure.

"There could be a reason for that," she said at last, fixing Sophie with a steady gaze. "Stipulations. Binding… agreements."

"Oh," Brianna said as if knowledge were blooming fully formed in her mind. Sophie was still frowning, but conceded Cynthia's point with a frown.

I alone was lost. I alone had no idea what anyone was talking about.

Miss Zenobia might have her reasons for choosing Brianna, who seemed like she would be wickedly brilliant if she weren't so off-balance, and for choosing Sophie, who was clearly well-educated and poshly sophisticated.

But me? I was a good server in the diner I worked in. The regulars liked me, and those stopping in off the highway as they passed through always took a shine to me as well. But I wouldn't chalk any of that up to "charm" in the way it meant next to the word "school."

The one special thing about me was a thing I had no control over.

"How did that get down again?" Mr. Trevor said suddenly, and got up from his chair to pick up the dark wooden box and set it once more on top of the hutch.

Really, what was in that box? The curiosity was driving me mad.

But if one of the others had moved it, I wasn't the only one fascinated with it.

CHAPTER 8

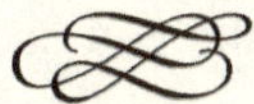

That bit of a nap had recharged me too much for sleep to take me. Well, that plus a renewed sense of purpose. I sat in the chair near the fireplace in my room, listening as the soft sounds of others moving in the rest of the house quieted. I waited a bit longer to be absolutely sure.

The voice in my head promised we weren't going to open the box. That would be breaking Mr. Trevor's rule. We were just going to touch it. Not just a fingertip on the very edge of the clasp, but a thorough examination. There was something odd about that box. I wanted to know what that wood would feel like under my palms. Was it as warm as it looked?

Curiously, I wasn't hearing any of the jazz music now. No Friday night party would wrap up so early. Perhaps Brianna was right, and I had been dreaming the whole time.

By about ten, I decided the house had been silent for long enough. I opened my door as slowly as I could, in case the hinges needed oiling. Then I was sneaking back down the stairs, still expecting those old steps to betray me with prolonged creaks or loud cracks, but they did not.

I reached the bottom of the stairs. No one was about. I looked down the hall past the dining room, but there was no light coming from the kitchen.

I felt a brief qualm. Was I doing the right thing?

No. No, I wasn't. Mr. Trevor had told me the rules. There hadn't been many, but I was about to break the most important of them.

What was I thinking? I felt like I had been sleepwalking. I gave my head a little shake, then turned to go back up the stairs.

Something behind me, at the end of that hall, rustled softly. Then there was a creak, a bit louder but still not alarming. Old houses made noises.

I put my foot on the first step.

"Amanda."

A woman's voice, but not Cynthia's. Not any voice I had heard before. It had been faint, but the summoning tone had been clear.

I looked up the dark stairway, then back over my shoulder again.

I had to know what was going on.

I turned away from the steps and crept down the hall, just as far as the doorway into the dining room. There was no one there.

The box sat at the head of the table. Who kept taking it down from its high perch?

Was I being punked?

Somehow, I didn't think so. Neither Mr. Trevor and Cynthia nor Sophie and Brianna struck me as the practical joking type.

Then another thought chilled me: had that rustle and creak sounded like a lid lifting?

It was shut now, but I had the sudden, unshakable feeling like it had been open a second ago when I had heard that voice. And if it had been open a second ago, what difference could it make opening it again?

I realized my hand was already lifting towards the box and snatched it back tight against my chest. What was happening to me?

I was giving myself the willies, that was what. I was being silly.

I had no business as a guest here wandering the house at night further than the bathroom. I hustled back to the bottom of the steps.

But once again, with my sneakered foot resting on the first step, I heard my name. This time the voice spoke out of the dark gloom of the parlor, but it was to my immense relief an entirely familiar one.

"Ah, Amanda. Please, do come in and sit with me for a bit," Cynthia said. I blinked, then finally made out her form. She was sitting in one of the two wing-backed chairs around the fireplace, but as there was no fire, she had blended with the shadows. Had she been waiting to ambush me, or did she just enjoy sitting alone in the dark?

"Was that you before?" I asked.

"Pardon?"

"Did you call my name a second ago?"

"Just the one time," she said, and I could hear the smile in her voice. She didn't seem to think I was crazy.

I wasn't so sure.

"Please, sit," Cynthia said, and she touched a small lamp on the mantle. It glowed with a soft, candle-like light.

I slid into the chair across from her. "Why are you sitting alone in here in the dark?" I asked.

"Oh, I was lost in thought," Cynthia said. "I didn't realize it had gotten so late, or so dark."

"Do you live here, in this house?" I asked.

"No, but I've spent my days here for so many years. I was fifteen when I first set foot in this parlor. This is where the group classes were held."

"When you were a student here at the charm school, did you feel exceptional?" I asked. Cynthia laughed.

"No, I did not," she admitted. "I didn't feel like I fit in at all, but Miss Zenobia took a special interest in me. She had seen me on the street and specifically invited me to attend free of charge. Me and my sister both. Our parents had once been well off, but money had gotten tight. It was an amazing opportunity for us."

"Opportunity to do what?" I asked. "It's just, I always heard of charm schools in the context of getting girls ready for marriage. But surely that wasn't something people were still doing when you were fifteen, in what, the seventies?"

Cynthia smiled. "It was a bit longer ago than that, but I take your point. Miss Zenobia's school was indeed precisely that kind of charm school on the surface. But she had a sharp eye for potential. If she saw one of her students was capable of more, she made sure that girl had everything she needed to go after her bigger fate."

"Like you being a lawyer?" I guessed.

"Precisely," Cynthia said. "I was the first woman in my family to pursue a real education. My parents didn't try to hold me back, but they didn't really understand me either. Without Miss Zenobia's guidance, I'm not sure I would have succeeded."

"I'm sorry I never got the chance to meet her," I said. "She sounds amazing, and it would have been nice to talk with someone who knew my mother. I suppose since I'm here for the reading of the will that my mother is mentioned in it. Do you know if there's anything about her, about her past, or something?"

"I'm sorry," Cynthia said with a shake of her head. "Not even I know what will be said tomorrow night. I only know I was sent to fetch the three of you, to be sure you were here tomorrow night."

"But if you were her lawyer, wouldn't you have helped her write this will?" I asked.

"It's not exactly what you're expecting," Cynthia said. "I really can't say more."

"It will make sense tomorrow night," I sighed, repeating that sentence I had heard far too many times.

"I know Miss Zenobia chose you three for a reason," Cynthia said. "She kept an eye on all of her former students and all of their offspring. Hundreds of them, and she was aware of them all. But only three were named. I don't know why, but I know you must all be exceptional."

"Exceptional young ladies," I said. "I don't feel like one."

Cynthia leaned forward in her chair to give my hand a squeeze. "Trust in Miss Zenobia. I promise you, she was never wrong. Now I really should be getting myself home to bed. Good night, Miss Amanda."

"Good night," I said.

I expected her to head out the front door when we parted ways in the foyer, but she walked down the hall towards the kitchen. She saw the box there on the dining room table and paused to put it back in its place on top of the hutch.

Like it was going to stay there this time. Somehow, I doubted it. I just hoped it wouldn't call out to me again.

I went back up to my room and climbed into the massive bed. The sheets were cool and soft and the blankets were so heavy it was like the bed was hugging me tight.

Still, I had trouble drifting off to sleep. Every time I felt my consciousness slipping away, some tinkle of noise would jolt me awake again. A pop like a cork from a champagne bottle, a stray bit of laughter, a woman singing something in a sultry voice.

But when I was awake, I heard nothing. There wasn't even a breath of wind to stir the trees around the old house.

Perhaps it wasn't surprising that when I finally did fall asleep, I dreamed I was at a party, sipping a cocktail made from bathtub gin and wearing a flapper dress and smiling at guys I was sure were gangsters because of their flashy suits.

Year of getting up to help open the diner before the breakfast rush had made me an early riser. I woke the moment the first ray of the rising sun pierced through the window. I had never pulled the curtains closed the night before.

I wrestled my way out of the twisted sheets and stumbled over to the window to look out at the back garden. Dew shone like diamonds on every blade of grass and branch of shrubbery.

The garden wall must stand at the very edge of a steep drop off, because the road behind it was quite a bit further down the hillside. Beyond the road I could see nothing but the tops of trees, the leaves not yet turning, although we were in the middle of September now.

I couldn't see the river through those trees, but I knew it was there. I bet in the cold of winter when the branches were bare I would be able to see it.

Another thing I didn't see: any sign of a party the night before. Mrs. Olson certainly hadn't been hosting one, not with all the complaining about noise she had been doing, and there were no neighbors behind us.

I suppose someone at the condo could have been hosting one, or maybe the whole building had a party.

If I ran into Nick again, I could ask him.

I really hoped I would run into Nick again.

I got dressed before heading downstairs to the kitchen. It couldn't have been much later than six, so I expected I'd be making my own coffee, but to my surprise there was already a potful waiting for me, a tray of mugs standing ready beside it.

I filled a mug, added a dollop of butter from the fridge, then carried it to what Mr. Trevor had called the solarium.

There was a crisp newspaper sitting out on the cast iron table and I could picture Mr. Trevor setting it out after making the coffee. I could even picture him ironing the pages like butlers used to do back in the day.

But the morning was far too lovely to risk ruining it with news. Instead, I strolled along the rows of plants clustered against the windows, sipping my coffee and trying to guess what all was growing. I recognized a few kitchen herbs, but most of the plants were a complete mystery to me.

I heard something skittering about outside the porch door. It sounded too big to be a squirrel. Raccoon? We had problems with those digging through the trash behind the diner. Just one raccoon is capable of making an ungodly mess. I set my coffee aside and opened the porch door, intending to chase away any creatures I might find lurking out there, looking for trouble.

But all thoughts of raccoons fled from my mind as I saw Cynthia crumpled on the ground at the bottom of the steps.

Face down. Unmoving.

The back of her head matted with blood.

CHAPTER 9

It was a good thing I had set down my coffee on the table in the solarium before stepping outside or else I would have done that thing people always do in movies. Drop and smash. Dramatic, but messy.

Although maybe the sound of the mug shattering would have snapped me out of the frozen state I was in. As it was, I don't know how long I stood there on the porch looking down at Cynthia's body.

Facedown, but with one hand reaching up to the top step, the hand gently curved. Like she was sleeping.

My gaze skittered away from the back of her skull. There was a definite curving in where it should be curving out, and my stomach flopped over even as my eyes refused to linger.

But I did notice other things. Like there was no blood on the ground around her, and there was no dew on her.

And her clothes were different. The last time I had seen her when she had been heading home for the night, she had been wearing black slacks and a cashmere sweater. Now she was wearing a dress. Royal blue where the blood spatters weren't staining it purple.

It reminded me of my dream from the night before. It wasn't

exactly a flapper dress, but there were a lot of similarities. Like it was a more conservative version of that style.

The sudden slap of a rubber-soled foot on concrete paving stone made me jump just as Brianna appeared around the corner of the house. She was wearing knee-length running shorts and a loose, white T-shirt over a sports bra, her long hair pulled up into a ponytail on the top of her head.

She nearly tripped over Cynthia's feet before she saw her, scrambling back to hug the corner of the house as she tugged earbuds out of her ears.

She stared down at Cynthia in horror.

Then she looked up at me.

"What did you do?" she gasped.

"Me?" I stammered. "I just got here. What did you do?"

"I was jogging," Brianna said. "This wasn't here when I left."

"I just got up. I haven't even finished my coffee yet," I said.

"So why are you outside?" she asked.

"I heard a noise," I said. I turned and looked at the back wall of the house. There was an old-fashioned light fixture over the door I had emerged from, aiming at the porch, but there was no sign of any home security cameras.

"No proof," Brianna said, as if guessing what I had been looking for.

"Who would do this?" I wondered futilely.

"She wasn't here when I left," Brianna said again.

"When was that?" I asked. Brianna pulled out her iPod and looked at the screen. "Thirty minutes ago."

"Exactly?"

"Thirty-one, then," she said. "I can't get it down to the second. I'm not sure when I came around the corner here."

"Why didn't you go out the front door?" I asked.

Brianna shrugged, her eyes on the ground around Cynthia. "This is weird," she said.

"Not enough blood," I said, nodding. "No dew."

"Secondary crime scene," Brianna agreed.

"What is going on?"

We both looked up to see Sophie emerging from between two shrubberies on the far side of the solarium.

"What were you doing in those bushes?" I asked.

"That's the door to the cellar," Sophie said with a dismissive wave. Then she saw Cynthia. "What's going on here?" She looked up at me and then at Brianna, eyes narrowing.

"We're trying to figure that out," I said. "Why were you in the cellar?"

"*When* did you go in the cellar?" Brianna asked, overlapping my own question.

"About fifteen minutes ago," Sophie said. She walked up until she was about as far away from Cynthia as Brianna and I were. She was as neatly dressed as the day before in gleaming sneakers, immaculate jeans of a deep indigo, and a silky tank top under a loose black cardigan. She gathered that cardigan closer around her, hugging her arms around her middle.

"Can you be more precise?" Brianna asked.

"No," Sophie said.

"But you came out this way and definitely didn't see her?" I asked.

"The cellar doesn't connect to the house anywhere," Sophie said, her voice inflectionless as her eyes never left Cynthia. "Those doors are the only way down there."

"Why were you down there?" I asked again.

Sophie didn't answer, and I didn't press her again. We all just looked down at Cynthia, the woman who had brought us all here from all over the United States, and we didn't even really know why.

And now she was dead.

Another voice pierced the morning air. She wasn't close enough for me to catch her words, but I would know that annoyed tone anywhere.

"Mrs. Olson," I said. "We can't let her see this."

"She's coming up the path past the dining room window," Brianna said, retreating from the corner of the house as if the neighbor frightened her.

"I'll get her," I said, jumping off the porch onto the grass and brushing past Sophie as I rushed to catch Mrs. Olson before she came around the corner.

"There you are!" Mrs, Olson declared as I appeared on the stepping stone ahead of her.

"Oh, you were looking for me?" I asked.

"Not specifically," Mrs. Olson groused. "I don't suppose Mr. Trevor is in?"

"I haven't seen him," I said.

"I thought as much," Mrs. Olson grumbled. "He's never in when I call."

"Can I help you with something?" I asked. I tried to take her arm, to guide her back to the front yard, but she twisted away from my grasp. For a moment, I thought she was going to hit me with the cane she was brandishing, but in the end she just used it to help her pivot and head back the way she'd come.

"I've already complained to you about the parties," she said as I fell into step beside her.

"Yes, you did," I agreed. "I heard them myself."

"Well, of course you did," she snorted.

"No, what I mean is, they aren't coming from this house," I said. "I was up all night on account of the noise too. It definitely wasn't coming from here."

"Well, it's coming from somewhere," Mrs. Olson scowled.

"It certainly is," I agreed. We had reached the steps that led up to the front door and she drew to a halt to turn and stare up at me.

She was tiny. I had thought she was taller, but when she had been talking to me over the hedge, she had been standing on higher ground than I had thought. The top of her head barely reached my armpit.

She planted her cane between her feet and tipped her head to glare up at me. "You can't put me off."

"No," I said. "I'm not trying to. I tried to figure where the music was coming from last night. I was up on the third floor. I could see pretty far from there, but I couldn't see any sign of a party. Maybe it's a trick of acoustics, sound bouncing from some other point in the river valley here."

"It's excessive," Mrs. Olson said.

"It was most of the night," I agreed. "You know, one of the other visitors here is a sort of scientist."

"The redheaded girl?" Mrs. Olson guessed. "She looked smart. Not particularly friendly. She ran away when I tried to talk to her."

"She's shy," I said, although I was pretty sure that didn't begin to describe what was going on in Brianna's head. "I'll talk to her about it."

"She can stop the noise with science?" Mrs. Olson asked skeptically.

"Well, maybe she can find out where it's coming from, and we can stop the noise with a complaint to the police department," I said.

Mrs. Olson just stared at me like I was nuts for a long moment.

Then she grunted and turned away.

"So, I'll get on that," I said to her back. She waved a hand over her shoulder, not turning back to look at me. If she said anything more, I couldn't make it out.

I went back to the backyard. Sophie and Brianna had stepped several feet away from the body and were talking together in low whispers.

"She didn't see anything," I told them as I approached.

"You're sure?" Sophie asked.

"She's just upset about the noise at night," I said. "The music and parties."

"I didn't hear anything," Sophie said with a frown.

"Me neither," Brianna said.

"I'm not crazy," I said.

"No, I don't think so," Brianna said. "Your room overlooks the backyard. Sophie and I both have windows over the sides of the house."

"It was pretty loud," I said. "Even with my window closed, I could hear it, all night long."

"It's an interesting problem," Brianna said.

"I'm glad you feel that way, since I kind of promised Mrs. Olson that you would look into it."

"Oh," Brianna said. "It's a little outside of my area of expertise, but I can take a stab at it, I suppose."

"I think we might be busy," Sophie said, pointing at Cynthia's body with her chin. "We have to do something about this."

"We should find Mr. Trevor," Brianna said. "I didn't see him when I came down this morning, but the coffee had already been made, so I'm sure he was up."

"He told me he likes to take walks in the morning and do some shopping," I said. "I'm sure he'll be back soon. But we should really call the police."

"No," Sophie said, exchanging a long look with Brianna. "We need to talk to Mr. Trevor first."

"Why?" I asked.

Brianna bit her lip and fidgeted with her earbuds as Sophie glared at her, practically daring her to say anything.

"What's going on here?" I demanded. "What did you two discuss while I was talking with Mrs. Olson?"

"I don't think we can tell you yet," Brianna said miserably.

"Yet?" I repeated.

"After tonight," Sophie said, and I practically screamed out loud.

"Now you two too? Everyone acts like this reading of the will is going to be like an instant education in everything. What on Earth is so magical about tonight?"

To my surprise, Brianna laughed out loud. And not a little bark of laughter, although it started that way. But when she put her hand to her mouth to try to contain it, the giggles just overwhelmed her. Soon she was bent double, hands on her knees as she laughed and laughed.

Sophie rubbed at her mouth with the back of her hand, but not quick enough to hide the grin that was spreading across her face.

"Really," I said, deeply annoyed.

"I'm sorry," Sophie said, and nudged Brianna hard in the ribs until she finally got herself under control.

"How can you be laughing now?" I demanded.

"It is funny," Brianna said.

"And I suppose I'll think so too at some point after midnight," I said with all the sarcasm I could coat those words with.

"Yeah," Sophie said. "Well, maybe not. I think part of it is contextual. Brianna's inappropriate emotional response to emotional stress."

"Yes, that," Brianna agreed, and all the merriment was back out of her in a flash. "I've never seen a dead body before."

"I have," I said darkly.

"Did Mr. Trevor give either of you a way to contact him? A cell number or something?" Sophie asked.

Brianna shook her head. I was about to insist once more that we call the police when, yet again, the sound of footsteps interrupted us.

Only this time, we didn't have enough warning to head them off.

And this time, it was Nick.

"Hey, there you are, Amanda," he said as he strolled around the corner of the house.

I'm not kidding. It was really a stroll, hands in pockets, super casual.

At least until he saw the body.

And the three of us gathered together on the other side of the lawn, not doing anything about it.

I really hoped he hadn't heard Brianna laughing, because just the dead body was going to be hard enough to explain.

CHAPTER 10

Nick looked down at Cynthia's body for a very long time, like he wasn't sure what he was seeing. He was dressed for jogging with earbuds dangling around his neck much like Brianna, but he didn't look like he'd started yet. Not a drop of sweat on him, and I could see he still had his car keys in his hand.

"We can explain," I said, and he glanced back up at me like he had forgotten we were there.

"We didn't do this," Sophie said, and something inside of me let out a sigh of relief that we were all on the same page on that, at least.

"We found her here," Brianna said.

"You were walking all around here," he said, pointing out the prints we had left in the sparkling dew. The rapidly evaporating morning dew.

"We didn't touch the body," I said.

"We didn't do this," Brianna said, repeating what Sophie had already said. Nick looked startled.

"I wouldn't think you had," he said. "Clearly this was done somewhere else, and the body was moved here."

"We thought so too," I said.

"None of you look like you've just been moving bodies around," he said, looking us each over in turn. Brianna's white T-shirt was sweaty enough to cling to her in spots, but not particularly mussed. Sophie looked like she had stepped out of a magazine shoot just a second before.

I, on the other hand, in my scruffy jeans and stained T-shirt from a concert I had never attended, looked like I was up for any sort of manual labor. It was the usual look back home, but not here. Did I look like I was equally up for pitching hay bales or for transporting corpses?

"I don't think any of you did it," Nick said, "but the fact is, this is a crime scene. Where you're standing now is good. Don't come any closer. Did any of you touch the body?"

"No," I said, and Sophie and Brianna also shook their heads.

"Have you called the police?"

"Not yet," Sophie said. She was cool, like ice cream wouldn't melt in her mouth. I waited for her to explain about wanting to find Mr. Trevor first, but she only spoke those two words.

"We just found her," I said. "It's been a bit of a shock."

"Well, I guess this explains Mrs. Olson," he said.

"What about Mrs. Olson?" I asked. "Did she complain about the noise? Because that wasn't us either."

"She said you three were acting odd. She heard you arguing and then when she came out to talk to you, you were behaving suspiciously," he said. I felt my cheeks flushing. I didn't want to be suspicious. "She's a bit overzealous, sees things where nothing is there. But I guess she was on to something this time."

"We should call the police," I said.

"I'll do it," Nick said, slapping his pockets until he found his cell phone. "Why don't you three go around that side of the porch to get back inside and just wait in the kitchen? I'll take charge of this."

"Why are you taking charge?" Sophie asked.

"I'm kind of police," he said, and this time it was his cheeks that were flushing red.

"Kind of police," Sophie repeated with a raised brow.

"Well, I'm going to be a police officer," he said, then amended again, "I'm going to start police academy in a few weeks."

"A-ha," Sophie said.

"I do have a friend on the force," he said, holding out the phone as if that could back up his story. "I'll call him now. Do you know the victim?"

"It's Cynthia Thomas," I said, remembering that he had said he had never met her. I was suddenly, profoundly sad by that realization.

It must have shown on my face. I felt a squeeze on my arm and looked over to see Brianna's eyes shining behind her cat-eye glasses. I squeezed her hand back, and she blinked the tears away.

Nick waited for the three of us to go back inside the house before calling his friend. I was sure there was a reason for that, but I couldn't summon the curiosity to really worry about it. I fetched my now-cold coffee out of the solarium and put it in the microwave to warm it up while Brianna and Sophie poured themselves fresh cups. Then we all sat around the kitchen table, looking down at the coffee we didn't take more than a few brief sips from.

A couple of cars pulled up first, and we heard voices in the backyard. A larger vehicle, I guess an ambulance, pulled up next, but at that moment Nick came in the back door with a man in dress pants and a tie, the sleeves of his dress shirt rolled up past his elbows. His hair was longer than Nick's, the thick waves on top looking like they would spring up into a pompadour if less attention were made to the careful combing and pomading that had happened not too long before.

"Everyone, this is sarge... er, officer Nelson Fisher," Nick said. "Nels, this is Amanda Clarke and... I'm sorry, I didn't catch your names?" His cheeks were flaming again.

"Sophie DuBois," Sophie said, and I would swear the accent that had lightened up this morning was back full force.

"Brianna Collins," Brianna said, her gaze focused somewhere in the middle of the table.

"I understand you are all guests for the weekend?" Officer Fisher asked.

"That's correct," Sophie said. "Our host, Mr. Trevor, stepped out before any of us were awake this morning and hasn't yet come back in."

"Would you like some coffee?" I asked, then jumped to my feet to fetch it before Officer Fisher could even answer. He and Nick sat down next to each other on the open side of the table and gave a nod of thanks when I set the coffee, then the cream and sugar, on the table in front of them.

"How well did you know the deceased?" Officer Fisher asked.

"I think we're all in the same boat," Sophie said, glancing at me, then at the top of Brianna's bowed head. "Cynthia Thomas came to see me about a month ago, to invite me here for this weekend. I hadn't known her or even heard her name before that day and had no contact with her after that hour or so over coffee until yesterday."

"Same," Brianna murmured. I nodded as well.

"Did anyone see her this morning?" he asked. We all shook our heads.

"I went out to jog thirty-one minutes before Amanda found her," Brianna told the table. "I ran down those porch steps. She wasn't there then."

"I went out to the cellar about fifteen minutes after that, and she wasn't there then either," Sophie said.

"You found the body?" Officer Fisher said to me.

"Only a second before Brianna came back from her jog," I said.

"Why were you outside?" he asked.

"I thought I heard raccoons," I said. "It was a skittering sound, like an animal. Not like someone moving a body. But when I went outside to chase the raccoon away from the garbage, that's when I found her."

Then Officer Fisher asked us a bunch of questions we couldn't answer. Really basic stuff like was Cynthia Thomas married, did she have kids or siblings, where did she live. It was more and more disheartening how little we knew about her. I could see Brianna retreating deeper and deeper inside herself every time she had to shake her head that she didn't know.

Sophie got haughtier and haughtier, and I was starting to sense that that was her own coping mechanism. What I had been reading as rudeness was just her being as stressed out as I was since she arrived the day before?

"When was the last time any of you saw her?" Officer Fisher asked. If our lack of knowledge was frustrating him, he didn't show it.

"Dinner," Brianna mumbled.

"Yes, dinner," Sophie agreed.

I felt everyone looking at me.

"I saw her at about ten last night," I said. "We talked for a bit in the parlor before she left. She said she was going home to go to bed."

"Did she seem odd in any way?" Officer Fisher asked.

"No," I said. "I mean, I had just met her so I don't know her very well, but nothing seemed off about her."

"And none of you saw or heard anything strange? Apart from a possible raccoon," he added.

Sophie's brown eyes bore into me, and I could tell she was silently urging me not to speak. Even Brianna finally looked up from the table to plead with me with her own dark green eyes.

What did they not want me to say? And why?

I didn't want to keep things from the police. What if the thing I held back was crucial to solving Cynthia's murder? I didn't know a lot about police work, but I'd seen enough TV shows to know even the smallest of details can become the clue that pulls everything together.

"There was music," I said. Sophie put a hand over her eyes with a sigh, and Brianna shifted her gaze back to the table. I guessed I had said exactly what they hadn't wanted me to say.

"Music?" Officer Fisher asked with a frown.

"That's been an ongoing issue," Nick said. "Mrs. Olson, the next-door neighbor, has been complaining about it since I met her."

"It's just, it's very old music," I said. "Jazz, but really old school jazz."

"Like from the jazz age?" Nick asked.

"I guess? I don't know a lot about music," I said. "But the other thing is, Cynthia's clothes were changed. When she left to go home to bed, she was wearing the same kind of slacks and sweater she wore when I met her before."

"Professional wardrobe," Sophie said. "Not corporate shark, all the right labels power suit kind of thing, but definitely lawyerly."

"Right," I said. "But when we found her, she was wearing a dress. Not like a flapper dress, but kind of similar? Like a normal daywear version of that."

"Jazz age," Sophie said, as if just realizing it herself.

"Or replica," I said. "We didn't get a good look because we didn't touch the body. But maybe there was a party near here? Some kind of blast from the past retro thing?"

"It would be the right neighborhood for it." Officer Fisher said. "I'll check into it. Maybe she lied to you about going home."

We all turned at an outbreak of noise at the back door. Then Mr. Trevor was there, clutching a grocery bag close to his chest as a uniformed officer led him to Officer Fisher.

"John Trevor," the uniformed officer told Fisher.

"Ah," he said. "Let's talk in the other room, shall we?"

Mr. Trevor gave a little nod. His skin was ashen, and I was afraid he was about to faint. I stepped up to take the bag from his arms and he murmured a word of thanks. And yet his eyes looked down at me like he wasn't sure if we had ever met before.

"Poor Mr. Trevor," Sophie said as I took butter and milk out of the bag and put them in the refrigerator. "He knew Cynthia longer than any of us. And Miss Zenobia, as well. I certainly hope he had other family and friends?" She looked to Brianna and me, but neither of us knew anything.

"Listen," Nick said, getting our attention. "You guys aren't suspects, but you might be needed for more questions later. I know you were only planning to be in town for the weekend, but you might have to hang around longer."

"Fine with me," Sophie said. "I brought everything I own with me."

Brianna bit her lip, and I could sense the torrent of words about her research and its crucial juncture that strained to explode out of her, but she held it all back and merely gave a nod.

"I should get going," Nick said, glancing at his wrist on which he wore no watch.

"The backyard is a crime scene," I said. "I'll walk you out the front."

"Thanks," Nick said. I led the way through the butler's pantry so we would emerge in the hallway on the far side of the dining room, where Officer Fisher was speaking to Mr. Trevor.

"I've always wondered what it looked like in here," Nick said, taking peeks into the parlor and up the stairwell and examining every photo that lined the hallway.

"Not a good time for the full tour, I'm afraid," I said. "Maybe later. Now that we'll be here longer."

"Yeah," Nick said. We had reached the front door, and I held it open for him, but he hesitated to pass through it. "I have to see to my grandfather and his dog now, and then I'm off to work, but I'll check in later if that's all right? See how things are going. If it's no trouble."

"No trouble at all," I said with all the smile I could muster. Having been a professional server for my entire working life, I should have been able to muster better.

"I'm sorry about your friend," he said. "I know you didn't know her long, but sometimes with some people, it just doesn't take long to form a bond. You know?"

I managed a better smile that time. "Actually, I do know."

He smiled back at me, then left.

The smile melted away from my face. What he had said was so true. I had known Cynthia for such a short amount of time, and really only had two or three conversations with her. And yet, I felt she had understood me. She had seen me, who I really was, and had liked what she saw.

I don't know what the future might have held. Maybe she would have been like a mentor to me. I could really use one.

But that wasn't to be.

When I returned to the kitchen, Mr. Trevor was there as well, and Officer Fisher had gone.

"Thanks for the help with the groceries," he said, and I could see he was still feeling numb. The other feelings were yet to come.

"Don't mention it," I said. "I'm so sorry for your loss."

"I have to tell her husband," he said, mostly to himself, but then he looked up at the three of us. "When you found her body, was she wearing her amulet?"

"Amulet?" I asked. "Do you mean that silver locket?"

"Yes, that," he said, and grasped my arm a little too firmly. "Did she have it?"

"I didn't see it," I said.

"She was laying face down," Brianna said.

"So it might have been there?" Mr. Trevor asked, his eyes wild.

I closed my eyes and brought the scene back to mind in every possible detail. I saw every wrinkle in her dress, every bit of mud-spattered on her shoes.

The gentle curve of the hand that had been extended up towards the top of the stairs.

"No," I said. "It wasn't there. I'm absolutely certain."

Mr. Trevor passed a trembling hand over his face. "That complicates things," he said, but didn't explain further. He turned to head for the back stairs, but there was at least one thing I couldn't go a minute longer without knowing.

"Mr. Trevor?" I asked, and he turned back to face us. "The reading of the will. Is that still happening tonight? Without Cynthia?"

"Oh, yes," he said. "Yes, nothing can change the timing of that."

CHAPTER 11

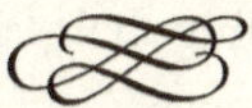

*A*fter Mr. Trevor went upstairs, I turned back to see only Brianna still in the kitchen with me.

"Where's Sophie?" I asked. "Did she go back out to that cellar?"

I couldn't imagine why she'd want to do that. Cellars that lurked under houses, only accessible by a door that didn't connect to the house, had to be nasty, spider-filled nightmares. That was why they called them cellars and not basements.

"I don't think so," Brianna said absentmindedly. "They asked us not to go into the backyard since it's a crime scene."

"Did she go upstairs, then?" I asked.

"Don't know," Brianna said, her mind even further away from me. "I need to check some things…"

She trailed off, getting up from the table and heading up the back stairs. I rinsed her mug and my own and set them on the rack, then hurried to catch up with her.

I could tell by her footsteps that she had stopped on the second floor and not the third, and sure enough, I found her in the library roaming the stacks as if she knew exactly where everything was.

"Did Miss Zenobia use the Dewey decimal system or something?" I asked.

"No," Brianna said, pulling a book down from a middle shelf, then moving further down the row and getting up on tiptoe to fetch a larger tome from a higher shelf. "Well, I guess you could say 'or something.'"

I looked around at the books, but so many of them were in languages I couldn't even sound out I had no clue how they were grouped. "I wish I could help you, but I don't think I can," I said.

"Oh," Brianna said, stopping halfway to the large table in the middle of the library with an armful of books. She almost looked up at me, but her eyes veered away at the last moment. "I usually work alone."

"Understood," I said, and backed out of the library.

Whatever Sophie was up to, she clearly felt the same way about the alone part.

Mr. Trevor was surely overwhelmed with tasks related to Cynthia's death. I had only known him a day, but I could tell he wasn't the type to contact the family and then step away from the rest of the work. And, not knowing anyone involved, there wasn't much I could do to help.

I went back up to my room, now blissfully quiet in the light of midmorning, but even after that largely sleepless night I was far too keyed up to nap. So I slipped my phone in my pocket and went out for a walk.

It was a gorgeous day, the sun bright and almost hot on my skin, but the breeze cool enough to give me a chill when I walked through the shadows of the many large trees.

We didn't have so many trees so close together where I lived. Most people had at least one tree somewhere in their yard, but here the trees were thick enough for their branches to thread together. If the street weren't so wide, they would be making a green canopy, a living cave for the cars to pass through.

I spent the whole day walking, walking down Summit Avenue until it ended in a park on the bank of the Mississippi. I strolled around the park for most of the afternoon before finally heading back to Miss Zenobia's Charm School for Exceptional Young Ladies.

I walked, and I looked at the houses and college buildings and people sharing the sidewalk with me, but I didn't really have thoughts going through my head. Not like word-thoughts. I just had feelings, mostly sad ones. Some anxious ones too.

When I got back to the house, it was still dead quiet. I made myself a cheese sandwich and a mug of tea in the kitchen and ate it alone at the kitchen table. Then I cleaned up what few dishes I had used and decided I could probably take a nap now if I wanted, after all that walking and sunshine.

And yet I didn't find myself heading up the back stairs. Instead, not remembering taking any of the steps in between, I found myself back in the formal dining room, looking up at the hutch.

The box wasn't there. It wasn't at the head of the table, either. I felt a strange rush of feeling—more than annoyance, bordering on outright anger—at its absence, but as soon as I tried to examine that feeling, it was gone.

I really needed that nap.

I could hear gentle rustling as I passed the second floor. Brianna in the library, probably.

I didn't even get my shoes off before I collapsed across the bed and fell into a deep sleep, undisturbed by party sounds or jazz music.

When I woke, the sun had nearly set, and I was hungry again. I tidied up my nap-head and went back down to the kitchen.

And still no one was there. Yet the unmistakable smell of chili filled the kitchen. When I switched on the light, I saw a slow cooker sitting out on the counter, a stack of bowls beside it. A note invited me to eat as much as I liked, and informed me there was cheese and sour cream in the fridge and biscuits in the towel-covered basket.

It felt weird, going about my business in this immense, silent house. And it was weird that it felt weird, since I had lived alone for years now. I ate alone, I curled up with a book in the silence of my little apartment, and I went to bed without saying goodnight to anybody. So this day shouldn't feel weird to me, and yet it did.

It was the house. The house so big it ate up every sound. The tap and scrape of my spoon across the bowl was muted, like I was eating underwater.

I wished I had one of those phones that had music on it. But perhaps that would be worse. The house would just consume the music.

Like it seemed to have consumed the rest of the people in the house with me.

After washing up my dishes, I decided I didn't want to go back up to my room, so I went into the parlor. While the library was filled with immense tomes, works I doubted I could understand even if they were in English, the parlor had a smaller bookshelf that was filled with novels. They were decades old, with faded covers and yellowed pages, but they were accessible. I found an Agatha Christie I had read only once before and curled up into a chair with it.

Then, as if under a spell, I promptly fell back asleep. I woke with a start when Mr. Trevor softly touched my arm.

"Miss Amanda," he said, and even in the darkness of the parlor I could see the grief etched on his skin. It gave my heart a little pang. "It's nearly time."

"Time?" I repeated, sitting up in the chair and sending the book on my lap spilling to the floor.

"Midnight," he said. "The others are already in Miss Zenobia's office."

"Oh, right," I said. "You found Sophie?"

"Yes," he said, giving me a puzzled look but not asking what I meant. I suppose, technically, I had never tried to find her. She might not actually have been hiding.

I followed Mr. Trevor up to the second floor and through the open door to Miss Zenobia's office.

A dim lamp glowed from the desktop, but the majority of the light came from the little fire crackling in the fireplace. Brianna and Sophie were already sitting in two of the three chairs that faced the desk, and they turned to look over the tall backs of the chairs as Mr. Trevor and I came into the room.

"There she is," Sophie said.

"Just in time," Brianna said.

"Miss Amanda, go ahead and get settled," Mr. Trevor said. I sat down on the last chair, then turned to look back at him and ask where he was going to sit. I thought perhaps on the other side of the desk, although it felt like only Cynthia should sit there and she was gone.

But Mr. Trevor was leaving, pulling the door shut behind him.

"Where are you going?" I asked.

"I'm not permitted to stay," he said. "This is for your ears only."

"But who...?" I started to ask.

"No time," he said. "I'll be back when the time is over."

I wanted to ask what that meant, but he was gone.

And then I heard the unmistakable sound of the door being locked from the other side.

"Why is he locking us in?" I asked, looking to the other two.

"I'm sure it's fine," Brianna said, but she didn't sound sure.

"But who is going to read this will if there's no one here but us?" I asked. Sophie shrugged, looking bored. I sat back in my chair to face the desk, searching the surface for some sign of paper or a computer tablet or anything.

All that was there, besides the glowing lamp, was the dark wood box from the dining room.

The grandfather clock sitting against the wall to my right began to chime. On the first stroke, Sophie sat forward and switched out the electric light.

On the fourth stroke, a wind picked up. The tree outside the window scratched at the glass and the wind seemed to swirl down the chimney, squashing the happy flames down to darkly glowing embers.

On the eighth stroke, the clouds parted, and the moon broke free, shining brightly through a gap in the tree branches to land directly on the wood of the box lid.

On the last stroke of midnight, I blinked. And in that instant my eyes were closed, the lid changed from opened to closed.

And a woman now sat in the chair across from us, the moonlight dancing all over her in silvery light. Her hair was done up in a style centuries out of date, and there seemed to be far too much of it for a woman of her age. Thick and lustrous despite its iron-gray color.

Her face was deeply lined, her nose sharp and prominent, but more patrician than witch. It was a stern face, like that of a queen who had been ruling despite the open disapproval of the men on her court for decades and decades.

Then she smiled, and looked at each of us in turn.

"Greetings Sophie DuBois, Brianna Collins and Amanda Clarke," she said. "I am Zenobia Weekes."

CHAPTER 12

$\mathcal{I}$ didn't know how the other two reacted to this announcement. I couldn't take my eyes off of Zenobia Weekes' silver-lit form to look.

"Sophie, I can see you share your mother's love of dance. There's such power in art, in beauty," Miss Zenobia said. Then her eyes moved from Sophie to Brianna. "Brianna. You've taken a different path from your mother's. A very different path. You're forging your own way. Impressive."

Then her eyes were on me, and I fought the urge to flinch away. The moonlight made her look ghostly, and the light reflecting off her eyes danced like little flames. "Amanda," she said, her voice so deeply sonorous it made my bones throb. "What can I say to you?"

She was silent for so long I was afraid she was waiting for me to say something, and I had no idea what it could be.

But then she clapped her hands together as if breaking the spell that held us all in thrall. "Time is short," she said. "I have much to tell you, and there could never be time enough for it all, so I must beg you not to interrupt with questions. You will have questions, of course, you will, but Cynthia will be able to answer those after my time is done."

"But Cynthia—" Brianna started to say.

"No questions!" Miss Zenobia said, and I had no doubts in that moment that she had been a teacher. Even if we had been thirty rather than three, we would have all fallen silent at that tone and tucked away the erasers and paper wads we had been about to throw before she could see them.

"I don't know how much you know, more's the pity," Miss Zenobia said. "So I will assume you know nothing. Your mothers were students of mine, classmates in fact. Very close friends. They were part of the last class I ever taught.

"I had many students over the years, and I helped as many as I could achieve their goals, whether it was getting an education in a world that had no use for an educated woman or if it was merely marrying happily and well to raise children a bit more open-minded than their peers. But that was just subterfuge. It was how I managed to pursue my real goal in plain view, but undetected.

"No, my real goal was to find the truly exceptional among my young ladies. The ones with very special skills. The ones I could take under my wing, to teach and to train, to mold them into the witches they were destined to be.

"But I didn't do this out of any sense of philanthropy. I didn't do it because I felt a calling to teach. I did it because it was absolutely necessary to have others who could take over after I was gone.

"I nearly failed. I know that. That last class... oh, time is so short I cannot tell you the whole story. But that last class nearly destroyed the work of my entire lifetime. It has taken decades and I still haven't repaired all the damage.

"Which is where you three come in," she said, looking back up at us with those flaming eyes. "I dearly wanted to meet you before I died, but it simply wasn't possible. I've been so seldom here, on this plane of existence. And the years have flown by. I dearly hope your mothers gave you some training, some preparation. They certainly should have appreciated the need for it.

"But I didn't live for better than two centuries relying on hope," she said with a wave of her hand. "Again, I must assume your mothers told you nothing. So now I've told you this much: you have a calling. You are all witches with a very specific task to be done. Witches like us have been tasked with such things throughout time. Guard this glade, keep this sword safe beneath a lake, protect this magic cauldron until the hero destined to take it arrives.

"We are called to protect this place. When I first came here, this was a barren ridge far from the hubbub closer to the river. Three times my home was destroyed, and I was forced to rebuild. In my great-grandmother's time, this place would have been declared a sanctuary, walled off from the rest of the world, but we witches don't have that kind of power anymore. I can't hide what lurks here within the walls of a temple or nunnery. Instead, I have to disguise it as a home. I can barely contain it."

She paused to pass a tired hand over her eyes, and I noticed the box still sitting on the desk before her. The lid that had blown open with the chiming of the clock was now poised in a position that was almost, but not quite, completely vertical. Even if the hinges were rusted enough to hold it at that angle, how had it gotten there?

"Where was I?" Miss Zenobia asked, hand still over her eyes. "Ah yes." She dropped the hand away. "What this house contains. Well, the house doesn't contain it. I did, with every ounce of my powers, and now it will be up to you to contain it.

"This place, more specifically the back garden of this place, is a focal point—a node, if you will—where the veil between here and beyond is particularly weak. Such places are prone to exploitation by those with the power, and this one is no exception. In this case, the veil has been torn just enough to allow a passage through time. It used to be unstable, random, but after decades of work I've locked it down. Both points are now fixed and travel through time together in parallel. Cynthia can explain about it more, for she was born on the other side but dwells on both. She has aged exactly as she should have, which is more than you can say about me. She will be my proof of what I say."

"But Cynthia—" Brianna tried to break in again, but Zenobia quelled her with a single raised hand and a furious glare.

"Time is short," she said, and this time I saw her looking down at the box in front of her. The box with the lid that was now halfway closed. It had moved again. Like the hands on a clock, always moving, but too slowly to be observed.

"I cannot collapse the time portal," Miss Zenobia said. "It's not possible. I made it stable; that's my final gift to you. But you must stand guard here. Time travel is not something humankind needs access to. It's barely safe for witches."

I leaned forward in my chair to look past the wings of the chair to see Brianna and Sophie's faces. But if they shared my inner freak out, they didn't show it. Sophie looked stern but resigned, like a knight accepting a quest they aren't sure they can fulfill but will gladly die trying.

Brianna, gazing steadily up at Zenobia's flaming eyes in a way she never managed with the rest of us, looked excited. No, more than that. Exhilarated.

I slumped back into my chair. What was going on here?

"The portal has been unattended since my death," Zenobia said. "I'm not sure how long that's been. If my calculations were correct, it should only have been a month or two. But even that time is too much. Incalculable damage may already have been done. You will have to look into it. My library will help guide you. But with no guard here for that time, things might have slipped through. Things might still slip through, if you are not diligent in your new task."

I heard a creak and saw the lid had moved further still, the very end of the clasp just brushing against the brass plate that was its home.

Something like fear passed over Zenobia's face, and my blood ran cold. I always thought that was just a cliche, but the icy chill coursing through my body was no mere imagery. I let out a breath that clouded in the air, swirling silver in the moonlight before fading away.

Miss Zenobia was looking fainter as well.

"Time is so short," she said again, and her voice trembled. "Centuries, but it went by so fast. Oh, my sister..."

Then she gave herself a little shake and looked back at us, the flames in her eyes as strong as ever.

"You have your calling," she said to us. "Now I need your solemn vow. Quickly now, for when the box closes, I will be gone, never to return. Swear!"

"I swear," Brianna said first, hands clasping together in front of her heart.

"Good," Miss Zenobia said with a nod.

I looked at Sophie, slouching back in her chair with her arms crossed like a teenager determined not to be impressed.

But then she sighed and sat up, putting one hand on her heart and the other in the air like a scout. "I swear," she said.

Then all eyes were on me.

"Amanda," Brianna prompted. "Swear."

"Swear to what?" I hissed back. "I don't understand any of this."

"You have to swear!" Brianna said.

"The box closes!" Miss Zenobia said, but her booming voice sounded like it was coming from the end of a very long corridor.

"Amanda!" Sophie said. "Swear!"

"I don't know what this means!" I cried, scrunching my eyes shut tight and pressing my fists to my temples.

I felt a touch on my shoulder and looked up into Sophie's warm brown eyes.

"Amanda," she said softly. "All that matters is that you want to do all you can to protect as many people as you can. In whatever way that you can. Can you swear to do that?"

I heard another little tap as the clasp on the box lid shifted, only the smallest of gaps remaining.

"We'll be with you," Brianna said to me.

"I can promise that," I said to Sophie. "Those words."

"Say that you swear!" Zenobia said. The tree scratched viciously at the window behind her, drowning out her words, and the clouds were swallowing up the moon. As the light faded, so did the ghostly form of Miss Zenobia Weekes.

"I swear!" I cried, leaping to my feet. "I swear, I swear!"

But she was gone.

Had I said the words in time?

Sophie stepped away from me and switched the desk lamp back on. Its light spilled over the dark wood of the box, now firmly closed.

"What did I just swear to?" I moaned. My legs felt weak, and I fell into the chair behind me.

"Just what you said you did," Sophie said.

"Is that what we all agreed to do?" I asked. "Just, what we can? Because it's crazy talk, most of what she said. I mean, clearly she was some kind of ghost, so I guess I believe in ghosts now. Who knew? But witches? That's a whole other thing, right? I mean, I guess some people in alternative religions call themselves that, but witches like she meant it, those aren't real. Right?"

Sophie and Brianna exchanged another one of those long, silent looks. The kind that were increasingly driving me mad.

"Right?" I said again.

"Actually," Brianna said, and I could see her cheeks flushing a pretty shade of pink.

Then I saw the wand in her hand. Where had she been keeping that?

"Yeah, we had the sense that maybe you didn't know, so Cynthia said not to say anything," Sophie said, poking the fire back to life. When she turned away from the fireplace, I saw she, too, had a wand in her hand. "But yeah, witches are real. And believe it or not, there are three of them in this room right now."

CHAPTER 13

I was still standing there with my mouth hanging open when Mr. Trevor returned. I heard the key turning in the lock and had a moment to pull myself together before he came into the room. He looked at each of the three of us as he slid the key away in his pocket, but when his gaze fell on the box resting on the desktop, I saw a tear in the corner of his eye reflecting the dancing light from the fireplace.

"Why couldn't you stay?" I asked softly.

"It was delicate magic," he said, then brushed past me to pick up the box. He clutched it tight to his chest, head bowed.

But somehow that box felt different to me now. It felt empty, if that makes sense, since I never opened it or picked it up.

"I have tea and sandwiches in the dining room," he said without looking up at any of us. "I'm sure you have much to discuss."

"She wanted us to talk about things with Cynthia," I said. "She didn't know she died."

"No, she wouldn't have," Mr. Trevor said, stroking the wood of the box with one finger. "I will answer what I can."

He went out of the room, and I looked to the others. They had put their wands away. Somehow, that was a bit of a relief.

"Delicate magic," Brianna said. "He doesn't know the half of it."

"I don't know any of it," I said glumly.

"I don't know much myself," Sophie said. "She created a hologram of herself or something? To talk to us after she died?"

"She preserved a part of her essence," Brianna said. "It's rare magic. No one I know back in Boston could do it, that's for sure."

"But you understand the concept?" Sophie asked.

"The rudiments," Brianna agreed. "She made an exchange: time from the end of her life for time with us."

"But not one to one, that exchange," I guessed. Because otherwise, it wouldn't be rare magic, I was sure.

"No," Brianna agreed. "I don't know the exact numbers, but it's more in the order of losing a year to gain five minutes."

"Why?" Sophie asked. "In a year, she could have just found us."

"I don't know," Brianna said. "And I don't think Mr. Trevor does either. Cynthia might not have even. She wasn't a witch like us. But we should remember that she did it. The reason why might be important later."

"Are we in danger?" I asked.

Sophie looked steadily at me, and Brianna shot as many darting glances up at me as she dared, but neither had an answer.

"I'm suddenly hungry," I said, hoping to break the somber mood. "Shall we?"

We all walked down the front stairs together, and I was sure we were all stepping as loudly as we could, coughing and clearing our throats, just to be sure that Mr. Trevor had plenty of warning.

But when we reached the dining room, he looked as cordial as ever, no sign of having hastily wiped his eyes or otherwise making an effort to pull himself together for our benefit.

The box was nowhere in sight. That was just as well. Even empty, it still freaked me out a little bit.

"My mother was mute my whole life," I said, the words bursting out of me. "She never spoke, and she never wrote anything down. I know nothing of her history before the day I was born. I don't even know her name. But I think if she had been a witch, I would have known it."

"Maybe not," Sophie said, taking the cup of tea Mr. Trevor had poured out for her and reaching for one of the sandwiches. "My mother was very insistent that neither of us ever show our power in public. I always thought she was hiding from something. I just never knew what."

"Past tense," I said, settling down with my own cup of tea. "Your mother died as well?"

"I believe so," Sophie said. "She disappeared when I was seventeen. I don't know what happened. One day, she just never came home from work. No one ever found a body or any evidence of anything."

"Did you ever try a locating spell?" Brianna asked, helping herself to one of each of the kinds of sandwiches and stuffing a peanut butter one into her mouth. Apparently, she was even hungrier than I was.

"No," Sophie sighed. "My mother taught me about feeling the flow of magic around us and through us. I can sense things that disturb it or things that influence it. For as long as I can remember, I've known to keep my feelings open wide, and if I felt anything like magical power, I would run as far and as fast as I could."

"Did that happen a lot?" I asked.

Sophie gave a little laugh. "I grew up in New Orleans. It's steeped in more kinds of magic than I have a name for. Yes, I've spent a lot of time running and hiding. I've gotten good at sensing things, and I've gotten really good at hiding inside the magic."

"You really have," Brianna agreed through a mouthful of food. "I wasn't sure if you were a witch or not until you told me and then dropped your guard. Then it was like boom! Full glow."

Sophie basked in the compliment for a minute, then took another sip of tea. "But that's all I know. Sensing and hiding. I never learned any actual spells. Although I'm sure my mother knew at least a few. She was always going to teach me, someday when we were safe. I guess we were never safe."

"My mother died when I was five," Brianna said. "But she was a member of a coven."

"What's that mean?" I asked. "Thirteen witches?"

"Yeah, but really, most of them only wanted to be witches," Brianna said. "But the two who really were witches took me in and brought me up. Sort of. They weren't really mom material. Not like my actual mom." She blinked hard, looking down at the still surface of her tea. "Well, maybe that's not fair. I wasn't what you'd call a normal kid. But they had lots of books. They showed me what they knew, but their books went so much further than they ever did."

"Could you do a locating spell?" I asked. "Can you help Sophie find her mother?"

"Not from here," Brianna frowned. "So far away."

"Maybe we could go there," I said.

"I'm afraid that won't be possible," Mr. Trevor said, and I nearly jumped. I had forgotten he was still there. "Not all of you, probably not even two of you, not for quite some time."

"No, we'll be needed here," Sophie said with a faraway look in her eyes. "I think I understand what I've been feeling since I got here. It's that time portal. It's… intimidating. No way I can guard it alone. It's going to need all three of us to do it."

"For now," Brianna agreed. "But if we study and practice and grow our skills, someday we'll be powerful enough to stand guard alone. Any of us."

"As powerful as Miss Zenobia?" I asked. I hadn't seen her do any magic beyond making herself into a time-lapsed ghost, but I was certain I would never be able to do even that.

"Probably not that powerful," Mr. Trevor said. "She had more than a century of practice before she even came here."

"Are you that old as well?" I asked, and Mr. Trevor nearly choked on his tea.

"Certainly not!" he sputtered. "I'm quite ordinary."

"So am I, I'm afraid," I said. "I've never felt a thing since I got here. I don't sense anything, or feel any flow, and I certainly don't know any spells."

"You heard the music," Sophie said.

"Mrs. Olson next door has been hearing the music for weeks," I pointed out. "She's not a witch."

"Not our kind of witch, anyway," Sophie said dryly.

"I don't think I'm going to be of any help," I said. "I'm afraid I might be the opposite of that. If the two of you have to compensate for me... I don't know. Wouldn't it be better to get another witch? Brianna says she knows a few."

"I don't know..." Brianna said, frowning down at her empty sandwich plate.

"There's being a witch, and then there's having the calling to guard this place," Sophie said. "I think they're two separate things."

"So I somehow ended up with a calling to guard here, but I'm not a witch," I said.

"We don't know that for a fact," Brianna said.

"How can we know it for a fact? Throw me in a pond, see if I float?" I asked, only half joking.

"I can check the library," Brianna said. "There must be tests we can administer. Real ones. Miss Zenobia must have had books on the matter."

"And there you go," I said, throwing my hands up in the air. "I'm already distracting you from the real work. If you're going to be searching the library for anything, it should be for information about what we're supposed to do with this portal."

"It's true. I know very little about it," Brianna said. "Although I don't think that will be a huge problem. My background in physics is going to be very handy, I think."

"We're going to have to live here," Sophie said suddenly.

"You already brought all your stuff," I pointed out.

"That was partly necessity, since I really did lose my student housing when I got cut from the master's program," Sophie said. "But it was mostly by way of protest. I didn't think I'd actually be leaving New Orleans."

She didn't say anything more, but I could tell by the way she was studying the crusts of her sandwich laying on her plate that she was thinking of her mother, and of how not going back to their home was as much as abandoning the search for her. Leaving her for dead.

Brianna was making a moaning sound, and I turned to see her rocking back and forth on her chair, hands fisted in her long red hair as she mumbled to herself over and over again. I could only make out a few words, words I'd been hearing her say since she got here. Research. Crucial juncture. Books she'd left behind.

"Brianna?" Sophie said, pulled from her own reverie.

Brianna's hands fisted even tighter, and I was afraid she was going to pull clumps from her scalp.

But then her rocking stopped, and she sat up. Still not quite looking at any of us, but at least she was calmer as she loosened her hands and smoothed her hair back.

"I'm fine," she said. "I can send for what I need. I can probably even still continue with my own program from here. My mentor is very accommodating."

"That's good," Sophie said, the end of the sentence lilting up ever so slightly towards being a question.

"I can't work from here," I said. "I don't know how the Schneidermans will replace me. Not that I'm irreplaceable or anything, but it's a very small town, and I look out for them like family. I mean, they have family of their own, but they all moved away..." I trailed off, realizing that none of those words were what was really in my heart.

"We need you," Brianna said. "I know we do."

"I know it too," Sophie said. "I sense that much."

"I don't sense anything at all," I said glumly. "I feel like if I stay, I'll just be wasting everyone's time."

"Miss Zenobia picked you for a reason," Mr. Trevor said, and I saw the hand resting next to his teacup had clenched into a tight fist. "You three. Each of you. That includes you, Miss Amanda. After everything she went through to find you and bring you here, after everything Mrs. Thomas went through..." he broke off, and I suspected he was choking back a sob. But he didn't give into it, just pushed his chair away from the table and started to leave the room.

He stopped in the doorway, hand trembling where he held the doorframe. He didn't turn back, but his words were quite clear.

"You have to stay. Miss Zenobia was never wrong. Never."

CHAPTER 14

We all went to bed at that point, deciding that further talk could wait until sunlight.

Not that I got much sleep. Every time I closed my eyes, the music and the party sounds grew louder still. It was like people kept sneaking into my very room to chat together and clink champagne glasses and dance the Charleston.

If I had been a real witch, I could have cursed all those partygoers. As it was, I couldn't even see them.

It's safe to say I woke up very grumpy. I got dressed and headed down the stairs.

I heard voices on the second floor and followed the sound as far as the library doorway. I thought at first Brianna was in there talking to herself, but when I peeked in, I saw two heads bent over that massive table and all the books spread open across its surface.

So Sophie was helping Brianna in her research. Apparently, she was not so confused by the plethora of languages as I was. That was just great.

I continued on to the kitchen and poured myself a mug of coffee, then carried it to the solarium.

The morning paper was there, ready for anyone who wanted to

read it, just as the day before. For some reason, that took the edge off my grumpiness.

Perhaps it just felt churlish, nursing bad feelings, when even Mr. Trevor, who had more reason to feel bad than I, still went about his job like it was any other day.

"Good morning," Mr. Trevor said as he appeared in the solarium doorway, coffee in hand. He raised his eyebrows questioningly, and I gave a little nod. As if he needed permission to join me.

Although, if I understood what had happened the night before, which I wasn't sure I did, I was now part owner of the house. Me, Brianna, and Sophie.

Somehow, that felt really unfair to Mr. Trevor.

"I see the others are at work already," he said, and I realized that Sophie and Brianna were in the backyard now, standing among the trees in the little orchard. They must have gone out the front; the back porch and several feet around it were still cordoned off with police tape.

"Did you help Miss Zenobia with her magic?" I asked.

"Not even a little bit," Mr. Trevor said. In contrast to me, his mood seemed downright sunny. "I tend to the house and garden and made sure she ate at least one meal a day, more when I could manage it. I suppose that sort of thing could be considered helping her with her magic. But it would probably be more accurate to say I freed her up to devote all of her time to it."

"What about Cynthia?" I asked.

"No, not her either," Mr. Trevor said.

"But she's from the other time," I said, waving a hand vaguely to where Sophie was now dancing between the trees, her arms making long, sweeping movements that felt very intentional.

"Miss Zenobia felt like Cynthia's mind could be put to better use here than in 1877," Mr. Trevor said.

"1877? That's what time it is?" I asked, confused. I didn't think the kind of jazz I kept hearing dated back that far.

"It was 1877 when they met," Mr. Trevor amended. "Cynthia was fifteen. She was eighteen when Miss Zenobia brought her forward in time to start college in 1971."

"And you worked for her, then?" I asked.

"My father did," Mr. Trevor said. "I took over for my father in 1980. But I knew Miss Zenobia in 1971, yes."

"This is kind of confusing," I said, rubbing at my head.

"It can be," Mr. Trevor said. "I don't know how Cynthia did it. She spent her days here, but her nights in the past with her husband and the rest of their families. I would find that so disorienting, but she never slipped up. Not once."

"Oh," I said, finally putting some obvious points together. "When she told me she was going home for the night, she meant her home back in…" I couldn't do that math.

"1927," Mr. Trevor supplied. "Yes."

"So," I said slowly, fidgeting with the edges of the pristine newspaper. "It's possible that she was there, in the past, when she died."

"No," Mr. Trevor said, but not as confidently as I would have liked. "No, I don't think so. She had an amulet, you see. She wasn't a witch with power to cross the portal on her own, but Miss Zenobia had created an amulet that let her pass from one side to the other. And when you found her body, you were very sure she didn't have it."

"Yes," I said, remembering every detail of that scene. "She didn't have it. I'm still absolutely sure about that."

I closed my eyes, recreating everything in my imagination. I guess it was a Zen thing because I couldn't try to do it. If I tried to, say, imagine the dress, I was afraid my mind would just conjure something up that would suit. But it wouldn't be correct; it would only seem correct.

No, I had to sort of let go. To not try. Like when you have a word on the tip of your tongue. The only way to remember it is to stop trying, to think of something else, and then it just appears.

Of course, for me, that usually happens hours later when I'm completely alone, and the word is no longer needed. But the concept still applies.

I heard Mr. Trevor sipping softly at his coffee and sensed he was giving me time to do whatever it was I was doing. Like he was respecting my process, even though he didn't understand it.

I could see why Miss Zenobia had kept him around.

"Her hand," I said, as something finally clicked. "She was holding her hand kind of closed, but kind of open. And it was up like she was reaching with it towards the house."

I demonstrated, straining out with one arm.

Mr. Trevor frowned. "You think she was holding it in her hand?"

"Maybe the clasp broke," I guessed. "But whatever the reason, after she was hit, her murderer took it from her." I took a gulp of my now-cold coffee. "Do you think it was why they killed her? To get her time-traveling amulet?"

"No," Mr. Trevor said with complete certainty. "No one knew that piece of jewelry had power. Cynthia was far too careful for that."

"So I guess she was just hit over the head and robbed?" I said, but then shook my head. "No, I thought her clothes were odd before, but it makes sense now. She was in 1927 when she was hit on the head. And the murderer moved her body to the back porch here, in 2018."

"But that's not possible," Mr. Trevor said.

Only this time, he didn't sound sure.

"What if it did happen?" I said. "Do you know what that means?"

"What does what mean?" Sophie asked as she and Brianna came into the solarium with coffees of their own.

"What were you doing out there?" I asked, waving my hand towards the windows.

"Checking the integrity of the spell that maintains the time portal," Brianna said as if she were describing me at the diner checking that the restrooms had enough toilet paper.

"Brianna can see it," Sophie said.

"Sort of," Brianna interjected.

"And I can interact with it," Sophie went on. "I can feel it and sort of flow through it."

"And when she does that dancing flow thing, I can see things swirl around her," Brianna said. "We found some places where the magic is fraying."

"That sounds bad," I said.

"It's good that we found them," Sophie said.

"I suppose that's true," I said. "Now what?"

"Yeah, I'm working on that," Brianna said, gulping down half her coffee at once. It was far too hot for such things if the tears springing in the corners of her eyes were any indication.

"But what were you saying when we came in?" Sophie asked me.

"Oh," I said, glancing at Mr. Trevor.

"Amanda is trying to solve Cynthia's murder case," he said.

"I was only raising some questions," I said.

"Like what?" Sophie asked, finding another chair in the depths of some ferns and turning it around to sit between me and Mr. Trevor.

"Well, the police said this was clearly a secondary crime scene," I said. "And if they can't find the primary crime scene, they don't have a very good chance of solving her murder."

"Yeah," Sophie said slowly.

"Oh," Brianna said. "Her dress."

"Exactly," I said. "It's the perfect crime, isn't it? The police here have the body, but nothing else. The police in 1927 have no body, so no crime to investigate, even though they have all the other evidence."

"Including the murderer," Sophie said.

"And the murderer has the amulet," I said.

"Amulet?" Sophie asked.

"The thing that let Cynthia travel between times even though she has no magic herself," I said.

"Was it spelled just for her, or could anyone use it?" Brianna asked.

"You can make something like that that only works for one person?" I asked.

"It's tricky, but well within Miss Zenobia's powers," Brianna said.

I looked to Mr. Trevor. He shrugged. "I never knew anyone but Cynthia to use it. But I don't know if she was the only one who could."

"I think we have to assume anyone could use it," Sophie said grimly. "We can have something like that on the loose. That's specifically what we're here to guard against."

"If we find that amulet, we'll find Cynthia's murderer," I said.

"Then what?" Sophie asked. "Like you just pointed out, the police force on either side of the time portal can't do anything about it."

"I don't know," I said. "We can figure that out after we've caught the killer. But we have to do something."

What I really meant was that I had to do something. I couldn't just sit around, watching Sophie and Brianna do all the work. And I couldn't displace Mr. Trevor just because our skill sets overlapped.

"A murderer and a time-traveling amulet," Brianna said. "Two things we can't leave on the loose. I agree."

"The crime is already a day old," I said. "I know that time is important in these things. Can we back to 1927 plus a day more?"

"No," Mr. Trevor said, although I had been looking to Brianna for the answer to that one. "Miss Zenobia used a huge amount of her power to make this portal stable. Both ends travel through time at the same rate. If you try to mess with that, you'll undo all that she did. No, you'll just have to start with a lost day. I'm sorry."

I nodded, then looked to Brianna again. "Can we jump back to 1927?"

"Yes," Brianna said. "I just need to check a few things in the library, but I'm sure that we can." She broke into a wide grin. "We can jump back and solve this murder. For Cynthia."

"For Cynthia," Sophie and I said together.

CHAPTER 15

$\mathcal{J}$t didn't take long for Brianna to find what she wanted in the library. She scribbled a few notes in a tattered and worn little book she took from her pocket. Then she put the book back in her pocket, gave Sophie and I both a nod, and we all headed back down the stairs.

Mr. Trevor was waiting for us at the bottom of the stairs. "Don't you think you're forgetting something?" he asked with a twinkle in his eye.

"I don't think so," Brianna said, pulling the book back out and mumbling to herself while she read over her notes. "No, I'm sure this will work."

Mr. Trevor looked at Sophie, then at me, but we both just shrugged.

"Come with me," he said, leading the way back up the stairs, past the library, past our rooms, to the attic.

The attic was long and narrow, only running down half the width of the house, with low, dim windows close to the dusty floorboards. Mr. Trevor flicked on a light switch, but the widely spaced bare bulbs didn't add much to the illumination.

"Cynthia knew you were coming, of course," Mr. Trevor said as he crossed to the back wall. If there had been windows here, they would have been overlooking the back garden. But there were no windows, just a line of cupboards built into the wall, the ones on the end shorter than those in the middle as the roof sloped down steeply from its central peak. "She made a guess to your sizes and brought back clothing for each of you. Those cabinets are for Brianna, these middle ones are for Sophie, and those two for Amanda. Take a look."

He had opened every door across the row, and we could see each was fairly stuffed with clothes from the fanciest of party garments to everyday work clothes for servants, even undergarments to match.

"These are like disguises," I said, touching the sleeve of what looked like a maid's uniform. "Did she expect we'd be spying?"

"She just wanted you to be prepared for anything," Mr. Trevor said.

"How do we know what to pick?" Brianna asked. "What time of year is it? What time of day?"

"It's mid-September there, same time of day," Mr. Trevor said. "Although September 1927 was unseasonably warm."

"Still a Sunday?" I asked.

"Yes," Mr. Trevor said with a nod.

"Church clothes?" I guessed.

"But we're not going to church," Sophie said. "We're going to be visiting people to ask questions."

"But maybe we should look like we've just left church," I said, pulling out a peacock blue dress. The color was eye-catching, but the cut was conservative. Or at least I hoped it was. I know some girls in the 20s wore some things that were considered pretty risque but would be considered tame now. But surely a hem that fell to mid-calf wouldn't send the wrong message.

Brianna found something similar in her closets in a lovely shade of pine green, and we both dug out shoes to match.

But Sophie put on something far shorter in the hem, plunging deeper in the neckline, with hardly any sleeves. The rosy material had a sheen to it and when she moved, it moved with her. Not in a clingy way, more like she had found the ideal dance partner in the form of clothing, and that partner was letting her lead.

"Are you sure?" I asked.

"I'm a dancer," Sophie said firmly. "This is what a dancer would wear."

"Mr. Trevor?" Brianna called. He had retreated to the top of the stairs, out of sight but in earshot. He poked his head back in.

"You all look lovely," he said.

"You don't think Sophie is inviting a lot of attention?" I asked.

Sophie held up her arms, then took a turn in a way only years of ballet could craft.

"Of course she is," he said approvingly. "Nothing she can't handle."

"Really?" I said skeptically. Brianna said nothing, but the little worried crease between her eyebrows said she shared my concern.

"Miss Zenobia's Charm School is well known in the neighborhood," Mr. Trevor told us. "A lot of little eccentricities can be explained just by telling people you are students there."

"That's all it takes?" I persisted.

"Well, people are going to think what people are going to think," he said, "but they aren't going to say what they're thinking unless they're willing to cross Miss Zenobia. Few are willing to cross Miss Zenobia."

Sophie arched an eyebrow at Brianna, and I gave up.

"If that's what you want to wear," I said, throwing up my hands.

It was kind of hypnotic, the way that skirt swished around her hips when she walked. A little voice inside me was regretting my choice, but I figured I would have an opportunity to try out some of the fancier things later when we weren't investigating a murder.

That, and I was pretty sure nothing in the universe was going to look as good on me as that dress looked on Sophie.

We went out the front door and followed the stepping stones to the back garden, giving the yellow police tape a wide berth. Sophie slipped off her shoes and handed them to me, then began a dance around the orchard. Her arms moved as she jumped and spun as if catching invisible ribbons to braid together in something far more complex than a maypole.

Brianna adjusted the glasses on her nose as her eyes stared into nothingness, her gaze unfixed.

"You see something?" I asked in a whisper. Which was silly; interrupting her was interrupting her.

"Yes," Brianna said. "It's like a tunnel, but it arches up that way like a bridge? Only it spirals back around too."

"Like a pedestrian overpass?" I guessed, but she didn't answer.

Sophie came dancing back to where we stood, then danced around us, her arms making little tossing gestures. Brianna flinched at one of them, then gave a little shimmy like Sophie had just tossed a ring over her head, and she was settling it down over her hips.

"Should I be doing something?" I asked.

"You're fine," Brianna said, eyes still unfixed.

"We've got you," Sophie said, and slid her hand into mine. "Spell time."

Brianna nodded and opened her little book. She began to speak in a deep voice, in words I couldn't understand. I couldn't even guess at the language. Sophie's hand clutched mine tightly, and I could feel her pulse quickening.

But I couldn't see or hear anything happening at all.

Then I blinked, just one blink, and all the trees in the orchard got several feet shorter. The wall behind the trees was darker, sooty like from a coal fire, but less chipped and worn than I was used to.

And the sounds of traffic down Summit Avenue that I had been tuning out without realizing it changed, the smooth running engines now sputtering and coughing as they lurched along.

"We did it!" Brianna said with a wide grin.

"You two did it," I said. "I was just along for the ride."

"Brianna did it," Sophie said, and Brianna's grin widened even more, although her eyes were looking down at her own toes. "Let's go in the house first. I'm curious who's there. Maybe we could meet Miss Zenobia."

"I think there are rules," Brianna said.

"Rules are for breaking," Sophie said, taking her shoes from me and sliding them on her feet before dancing up the steps to the solarium door.

"Not the rules of physics," Brianna said, but Sophie had already gone inside.

Brianna and I followed her in, past the kitchen and dining room, to the front parlor. There were lots of little changes. The appliances in the kitchen were either gone or replaced by more rudimentary versions of the same. The furnishings were different, although equally fine.

But no one seemed to be home.

"I think there are patterns," Brianna said, turning pages in her little book. "I need to do more research."

"But we went so far back in time, it's not like we'd ever meet ourselves or anything dangerous like that," I said.

"We could meet our great-grandparents," Sophie said.

"I think it's more complicated than that," Brianna said.

"So we can't change things in the past?" I asked.

"Well," Brianna said. "We can, but only because we already did, because we're part of the past now."

I rubbed at my forehead and pondered whether I even understood that.

"It doesn't matter," Sophie said. "We'll figure out what's impossible when we try to do it. In the meantime, we need to find Cynthia's husband. Statistically, he's the most likely suspect."

"Oh, I don't know," I said. "If it was a domestic thing, why move the body and steal the amulet?"

"It's the logical place to start," Sophie insisted.

"I suppose so," I said. "He might be innocent, but talking to him and seeing Cynthia's home will give us leads on where to go next."

"I should have found a directory to 1927 St. Paul in the library before we came," Brianna said. "I didn't even think to look. I'm sure she must have had one."

"No worries," I said, opening the front door and leading the way out onto the front porch. "We can ask around until we find it."

"Ask who?" Brianna said.

"Ask what?" someone else said excitedly. I looked around until my gaze fell on a girl of about twelve sitting at the base of the much smaller oak tree in the front yard. She was wearing what was likely her Sunday best but sitting in dark earth that looked like someone had been planting bulbs in it perhaps the day before. Her black hair was cut in a bob, but the bangs were too long and kept falling into her eyes and yet not long enough to stay tucked behind her ear, although her fingers kept trying to make that happen.

"Hello, little girl," I said. "What's your name?"

"Clotilde McTavet," she said, getting to her feet and holding out her hand to shake. "But you can call me Coco."

"Hello, Coco," I said.

"You're new students?" she surmised. "I've not seen you around before."

"Yes, we are," I agreed. Not even a lie. "I'm Amanda, and this is Brianna and Sophie. We're looking for Cynthia Thomas."

"She's usually around," Coco said, looking past my shoulder as if expecting to see her lurking on the porch or peeking out of one of the windows. So her death wasn't yet common knowledge here. I wasn't sure what that meant.

"Do you happen to know where she lives?" I asked.

"How do you not know where she lives if you're students here?" she asked, eyes narrowing suspiciously.

"We're new," I reminded her.

"Still," she said. "Maybe you should just wait for her to come back."

Sophie gave an exasperated sigh, which I ignored. "Coco, I'm sorry, but Mrs. Thomas has died," I said.

"Died?" Coco repeated. "How?"

"Murder, I'm afraid," I said. "We really need to talk to her husband—"

"Murder!" Coco said with perhaps too much glee. "Do you know who did it?"

"No," I admitted.

"But you have a list of suspects?"

"No," I said.

"We're new," Sophie said. "We don't know anyone."

"Well, I know everyone," Coco said. "I could help you."

"Directions would be nice," Sophie said, but Coco continued on as if she hadn't heard.

"Do you know who I'd start with? Old Mr. Brown," she said in a conspiratorial whisper. "He hates everyone, of course, but he particularly hates Miss Zenobia and the students of her school."

Brianna whipped out her little book and wrote that name down.

"He's just over there," Coco said, eying Brianna's scribbling pencil as she pointed past us to Mrs. Olson's house. Apparently Mr. Brown's in 1927.

"Thanks for that tip," I said. "But Mr. Thomas—"

"Or!" Coco said, throwing up her hands in something too much like jazz hands for the matter under discussion. "Just a block that way is the hotel where F. Scott Fitzgerald used to live before he hightailed off to New York and Paris. And do you know who stays there now? Tons and tons of bootleggers. Gangsters!"

"Why would gangsters kill Cynthia?" Brianna asked, her pencil poised over the page of her book.

"They kill all sorts," Coco said in a worldly voice. "It's worth looking into."

"It might be," Brianna said and made a note.

"Ooh, another thing?" Coco said, waving us to bend our heads closer to hers. "There are pirates that hide in the caves down by the river."

"That sounds like Tom Sawyer," I said, then tried to remember when that book had come out.

"But these are real, not just a story," Coco insisted. "I've been wanting to explore the caves forever, but my mother says I can't go. I guess sometimes kids get lost and die down there, grownups too, but I'm smarter than most people, so I think I'd be just fine."

"I think you should listen to your mother," Sophie said, and Coco scowled at her before turning her attention back to me.

"If you go, take me with you? I could be your guide!"

"How can you be our guide if you've never been down there before?" Sophie asked.

"I know stuff," Coco said sullenly. "I've listened to all the stories, and I've gotten my hands on all sorts of maps. I know more about it than anybody."

"A-ha," Sophie said skeptically. Coco looked like she was going to snap back when the sudden calling of her name made her whole body stiffen.

"Clotilde McTavet, I hope you're not bothering those nice ladies," a young man said as he came down the steps of the house next door.

A house standing on the lot that was condos in 2017. I wondered what had happened to it. It was massive, twice the size of Miss Zenobia's Charm School, although not in a Queen Anne style. It had more of the solid, straight line look of something Greco-Roman.

Yeah, I don't know much about architecture.

Coco turned to face the young man, trying to wipe the dark earth from the back of her skirt surreptitiously.

"I wasn't bothering," Coco said.

"She wasn't," I said.

"Well, you weren't tending to the errand your mother gave you either, were you?" he asked. The words might be chiding, but the twinkle in his dark brown eyes and the way he leaned a shoulder against the tree rather than lording it over Coco took a lot of the edge off.

"I'll get to it," Coco said.

"You should get to it now, or you'll be in trouble again," he said. "Go on. I've already covered for you once when your mother asked if I could still see you in the yard."

"I wasn't in our yard," Coco pointed out.

"So you and I know I wasn't lying, but we also both know your mother isn't going to see it that way," he said. "Get along now."

Coco scowled, but she patted her pocket as if to confirm it still contained something, then started down the sidewalk at a brisk trot.

I was a bit sorry to see her go. She wasn't the most cooperative of informants, but she was a far sight better than nothing, which was what we had now.

CHAPTER 16

$\mathcal{B}$rianna was looking over her notes, tapping next to each item with the tip of her pencil and frowning. Sophie was watching Coco disappear down the sidewalk. Then she turned to say something to me, and we both noticed the young man was still there, leaning against the oak tree.

"Can I help you?" I asked.

"I was wondering if I could help you," he said. "The name's Edward Scott."

"Amanda Clarke," I said. "This is Brianna Collins and Sophie DuBois."

He touched the brim of his hat at each of us. "Given where we're standing, I'm guessing you're new students at Miss Zenobia's school?"

"We are," I said. "Everyone seems to assume that about us. I would have thought most of her students were local."

"Most are," he said. "You're definitely not. All three of you have a bit of a glow, like you're from somewhere absolutely fabulous." He raised his eyebrows inquiringly.

"New Orleans," Sophie said, extending her hand to him. Just two words, but I could hear how she kicked her accent up to maximum power. And from the way he kissed her hand and murmured he was charmed to meet her, I could see it had had its effect.

"We're looking for someone," I said. "I don't suppose you could tell us the way to the house of Mrs. Cynthia Thomas? I'm afraid we don't know her husband's first name."

"I can do you one better," he said with the barest hint of a wink. "I can show you. It's not far."

He held out his arm to me, and I took it. With Sophie still holding his other arm, we started down the wide sidewalk, Brianna with her nose deep in the pages of her book trailing along behind.

"Scott, not McTavet?" I said to him as we walked. "So you're not Coco's brother."

"No, I was there to call on her older sister Ivy, but she isn't entertaining visitors yet," he said.

"It is awfully early," I said.

"I suppose," he said wistfully. "But when we met at the Hills' do last night, I thought we'd really made an impression on each other. I woke up at dawn itching to see her again."

"Maybe she just doesn't want to seem too eager," I said. Edward certainly wasn't having that problem.

"I reckon you're right," he said with that little flutter of his eye that was almost but not quite a wink.

We took a turn off of Summit Avenue, heading north away from the ridge and the river. The houses here were a bit smaller, a bit less swank, but still far beyond anything I'd ever seen back home.

"Here we are," Edward said, drawing to a halt where the front walk of a Tudor-style house met the sidewalk. "Mr. Frank Thomas, husband of Cynthia Thomas. I believe her maiden sister Helen lives with them as well."

"Thank you so much," I said. "This has been very helpful."

"Think nothing of it," he said with another touch of his hat.

We climbed the steps of the front porch, Brianna finally extricating herself from her book and putting it away in her pocket. Sophie rang the bell in that firm way she had, and we waited.

A few minutes later, Sophie rang again.

Sophie was just looking to Brianna and me in silent inquiry of whether a third ringing would be of any use when the door finally swung open.

I could see Cynthia in the woman that stood looking dully out at us, but it was a worn, badly used version of Cynthia. Her hair was long and in disarray, slipping out of its updo everywhere. The dress looked like good quality, but it was negligently worn, sitting askew on her shoulders and badly wrinkled.

The woman just looked out at us without saying a word until Sophie couldn't take it anymore.

"We're from Miss Zenobia's school," she said. "Is Mr. Frank Thomas in?"

"Miss Zenobia," the woman said with distaste, but stepped aside to allow us to pass into the foyer.

"You've gotten the news?" I asked anxiously.

"Yes, we've gotten the news," she said. "Such a way to get news, I really don't know."

I didn't know what to say to that, so instead, I said, "you're Cynthia's sister?"

"I was," she said. "I'm Helen."

"We're so sorry for your loss," I said, but she didn't respond. I guessed she was the type who would go numb first. She certainly looked as if she was not eating or sleeping properly. Was there no other member of the family to help out in their time of grief?

We stopped outside a darkened parlor. I bet the place was cheery in normal circumstances, but on this morning someone had pulled closed the heavy curtains, blocking out every bit of the unseasonably warm September sunshine. It took a moment for my eyes to make out a human-shaped form in one of the chairs, all but lost under the folds of a gray wool lap blanket.

"Frank," Helen said, and her voice had a softness it had been lacking before. "You have visitors if you're up to it."

Frank stirred, head raising from a hand that had been pressed to his forehead. He braced to rise up out of the chair, but I hastened forward.

"Please, there is no need for formality," I said. "We're students from the school."

Frank sank gratefully back into his chair, then looked at each of us in turn with watery eyes. "Of course you are. Thank you for coming. I thought, perhaps given the circumstances, no one would be able to."

I exchanged a look with Sophie and Brianna. Did he know of the existence and subsequent theft of the magic amulet?

"You knew my Cynthia?" he asked, squeezing my hand.

"All too briefly," I said. "My name is Amanda Clarke, and this is Sophie DuBois and Brianna Collins."

"Pleased to meet you all," he said. "Helen, could I trouble you with making a spot of tea?"

"I've already put a kettle on," Helen told him from the doorway.

"She was a most extraordinary woman," Frank said. "She lived a most extraordinary life. How could it all end this way?" He pressed a trembling hand to a forehead that was already red from too much pressing, but even that gesture didn't seem to be enough. I stepped back as she rose up out of the chair again. "Excuse me. I must tend to a… Please, excuse me."

He retreated to a door on the far side of the parlor and closed it behind him.

"Poor dear," I said.

"He seems awfully cool with Cynthia's… lifestyle," Sophie said. "Do you think he even knew she traveled through time every day when she went to work, or did he just think she was there in the house working for Miss Zenobia?"

"He knew," Brianna said, picking up a scrap of paper from the table next to Frank's chair. It was a telegram from a woman named Tabitha Smythe in London. JOHN TREVOR REGRETS TO INFORM YOU OF CYNTHIA'S DEMISE. DETAILS TO FOLLOW.

"How horrible," I said, looking up at the other two. "Such a cold way to get such news. No wonder Helen was so upset about it."

"Who's Tabitha?" Sophie asked.

Brianna shrugged. "We can ask Mr. Trevor when we get back. My bet is that she's a witch in our time who has access to a portal of her own and went back in time to send this telegram. Without the amulet, Mr. Trevor couldn't send word himself."

"I guess not," I said.

"What do we do now?" Sophie asked.

"I don't think he did it," I said. "He seems genuinely grief-stricken."

"He could be and still be the murderer," Sophie said. "Maybe it was some kind of accident."

"That ended with him stealing her amulet and moving her body? I don't think so," I said.

"We can ask him questions," Sophie said.

"We're not interrogating a grief-stricken old man," I said. Something in the way he had grasped my hand spoke of pain, not the pain of loss but a deeper, chronic pain long lived with. Maybe a form of arthritis, like Mrs. Olson.

"We don't have to," Brianna said. "I can do a spell."

"A guilty or innocent spell?" Sophie asked.

"Not exactly. I know a way to see if oaths have been broken," Brianna said. "I just need his wedding band for a moment."

"That's kind of a big ask," I said.

"I can get it," Sophie said. "And I can keep him occupied while you do your spell, provided you can do it here."

"I can," Brianna said.

"I'll stick with Helen," I said. "Give me a sign when you're done."

The door at the far side of the parlor creaked open, and Brianna gave me a swift nod. Then she and Sophie turned their attention to the returning Frank.

I slipped out into the hallway and listened for a moment. I could hear the soft sounds of cups and saucers being laid out on a tray and followed it to find Helen alone in a massive kitchen.

"Hello," I said. "Do you need any help?"

"I'm fine on my own," she said, adding a small pitcher of milk to the tea tray.

"I would have expected that a house this size would have a large staff to help run it," I said.

"It's Sunday," Helen said, as if that explained it. I suppose it did.

"Still, you look very at home in the kitchen."

"I'm not the lady of the house," Helen said.

"No, I guess that was Cynthia," I said. "I only knew her a short time, but she didn't strike me as a kitchen sort of person."

"No, she certainly was not," Helen said.

"Being a lawyer is a time-consuming profession," I said. "I'm sure she was grateful you were here to help with the tasks she couldn't attend to personally."

"Tasks she considered beneath her," Helen said with a sniff. The kettle on the stove began to whistle, and she used the end of her apron as a potholder to lift it and pour the water into the waiting teapot.

"I'm not sure she felt that way," I said, and Helen scowled and turned away from me to put the kettle back. "I never understood people who did, though. Home means warmth and comfort, good food and clean clothes and soft beds. None of that comes without work, but what work could be more meaningful than making a home?"

"Cynthia never saw it that way," Helen said. "Always had something more important to be doing. I blame that Miss Zenobia, putting ideas in her head."

"I don't know that Miss Zenobia was wrong," I said. "Cynthia was a very good lawyer."

"Maybe," Helen allowed. "But she should have set it aside when she married. And now she's corrupting our maid, Molly, filling her head with ideas above her station. She barely gets her work done, spends all of her time with her nose buried in my sister's books. She's never even met Miss Zenobia, but still that woman's influence is going to ruin her life. She's never going to have what she wants. Poor girl," she added in a kinder voice.

She felt sincere to me. She genuinely believed that a maid wanting to be more than a maid was cursing herself to a lifetime of unhappiness. I kind of wanted to argue that point, but that wasn't why I was here.

"Were you a student of Miss Zenobia's as well?" I asked instead.

Helen looked like she didn't want to answer at first. Then she sighed and nodded. "Not one of the exceptional ones. Not in her eyes. I was never good with being charming, that's the truth. I don't flatter, I speak my mind, and I've never been much of a looker."

"Everyone has a talent," I said. Helen shrugged, then turned to open the heavy door of the icebox. She reached for a container of clotted cream, but something on the bottom shelf caught my eye.

"What a lovely marble rolling pin," I said. "I've never used one myself, but I've heard they're marvelous for rolling out thin dough."

"It's handy," Helen said grudgingly. Then, as if the words were being dragged out of her, she added, "it was a gift from my sister."

"Those are from France, right?" I asked.

"I guess, but she got it from that other place she goes," Helen said. "You know."

"I think I do," I said evasively.

"You know, because you're from there too," Helen said with a sniff and put the cream back in the icebox. "The future."

"I would've thought a gift from the future would be against the rules," I said.

Helen scoffed. "Well, she did tell me to keep it secret. That, and the other things she brings me. Cookbooks I have to commit to memory so she can take them back. Ingredients I can't get here."

"That was good of her," I said.

"The baking was all mine," Helen said fiercely. "I didn't need all that to make the best food for miles around. She doesn't get credit for that."

"No," I agreed, but she plowed on as if she didn't hear me.

"She always wanted all the credit for everything, making me keep secrets for her. I never married because how could I? So many secrets I would have to keep for her sake, how could I marry with so much dishonesty before I even took my vows? I couldn't. I didn't. But between you and me, without her, I would have married well. I might not be pretty or charming, but I could run a household ten times this size, and it'd run like clockwork. Many men value such things."

Despite her bragging words, she seemed to be having trouble finding something in the kitchen. She kept opening and closing cupboards, the same ones over and over, and running her hands over the counters.

"Can I help you find something?" I asked.

"I know this kitchen like I know my own mind," she snapped.

"I'm sure you do," I said. "But you've had a terrible shock, and that takes a toll. Let me help you."

She looked like she wanted to argue, but then her shoulders slumped.

"It's not the shock," she said. "It's Molly. She keeps moving my things. I'll have to speak to her in the morning."

I looked down at the tea tray. Everything seemed to be in its place. Then I noticed the sugar bowl was empty. "Sugar?" I guessed.

"It's in a canister, but none of these," she said, lifting the lids off of the canisters lined up by size on the counter. I had seen her do that twice before and not find what she was looking for.

I was just thinking that perhaps Brianna could try that locator spell of hers when I spotted the glint of something lurking behind the decorative wood topper of the hutch. "Is there something up there?" I asked.

Helen took a moment to find what I was pointing at, then frowned as she pulled a chair over to the hutch and stepped up onto it.

Another way she was different from her sister: Cynthia had been thin, almost too thin, but Helen had thick arms and chunky legs. She planted one solid foot on the seat of the chair and stepped up to peer over the top of the hutch.

"Here it is indeed," Helen said, stepping back down with the little canister in her hand.

"Kind of an odd place for it," I said, fighting the urge to brace myself as Helen lifted the lid. She poured a glistening stream of sugar into the bowl, and I had to tell myself that not every container left tucked away on top of a hutch contained the ghost of someone's soul.

Helen hefted the massive tray and carried it into the parlor. As she poured out tea for all of us, I chanced a little glance at Brianna, then at Sophie.

Brianna tipped her head Frank's way, then gave it a little shake.

So Frank was free of blame. And Helen certainly had a lot of conflicting feelings about her sister, but that was perfectly natural. A time-traveling older sister who became a lawyer and still managed to marry well would irk any little sister with more mundane skills and no husband to show for it. But surely not enough to kill her over.

And there was still the matter of the amulet. Helen would have known what it was, knowing what her sister could do. So why would she take it, then not use it to get to the future?

Suddenly, I felt a cold chill run up my spine. If the murderer had known what the amulet was when they had taken it, why would they linger in 1927?

Were we looking in the wrong time?

CHAPTER 17

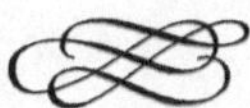

e took tea with Frank and Helen, trying not to stuff ourselves on the little cakes and tarts, which wasn't easy. Helen might brag herself up a bit, but she didn't exaggerate.

Frank told us all about how he had met Cynthia (one of a line of charm school girls at a society function), about their long courtship (she had been attending college at the time, unbeknownst to him), how he finally got her to agree to marry him on the third proposal, and all about their happy albeit childless life together.

It was clear that he had adored her. It was also clear he had a pretty hazy idea of what it was she did all day. It was like his mind just skated over the fact that she traveled to the future every day after she kissed him goodbye and before she returned in the evening.

We were in that parlor for more than an hour, and no one had ever opened up the curtains, so when we found ourselves back out in the bright September day, we had to stop at the bottom of the porch steps to blink and adjust our eyes.

"Oh, he's still here," Brianna said, and I looked up to see Edward Scott loitering against a tree on the other side of the road. He saw us looking at him and gave a little wave, then crossed the street.

"I thought I'd walk you back," he said.

"Did you think we wouldn't find our way back?" Sophie asked.

"Not a bit," he said amiably. "But if Ivy is up now and looking out her window at the street, perhaps seeing me escorting three lovely ladies past her house will give her a twinge of regret for turning me away earlier."

"I don't know if I want to be a part of anything so manipulative," I said.

"Would it help to know that I saw her looking out the window when I came to her house before, and I know for a fact she was out of bed but told her maid to say she wasn't?" he asked. "And if you still don't believe me, we can ask Coco. She'll back up my story."

"Coco is fond of you," I guessed. "She'll back you up no matter what you say."

He tipped his head to look at me out of the corners of his eyes. "This is true. You're very astute." Then he held out his arms to Sophie and me. "Shall we?"

I exchanged a glance with Sophie, and she gave a careless shrug. We were going that way, anyway.

"Speaking of Coco," Edward said as we walked. "She came by while you were inside with Mr. Thomas and told me what happened to Cynthia. You have my deepest condolences."

"Thank you," I said. "But we only knew her for a short time."

"Do the police have any leads?" he asked.

"I don't believe so," I said, quite certain the police in this time didn't even know that a crime had been committed.

"Coco has a long list of suspects," Edward said.

"We know," I said.

"Probably longer than you know," he said. "I think she's been adding to it since you talked with her last. She's very excited. I tell you this by way of warning; she's going to want to help out. I believe she's actively searching for you to offer her services."

"We'll keep an eye out," Sophie said.

"She seems a fanciful girl," I said. Then, in case that sounded too harsh, I added, "I quite like her."

"Ditto on both scores," Edward said. "But she did have one name on that list that could be a real possibility."

"Oh?" I said, looking back over my shoulder to be sure Brianna was following close enough to hear him. Not only was she right behind us with her little book open, she had the pencil poised to note down what he said next.

"Yes," he said. "I think we can agree that gangsters and pirates are probably not likely suspects, but Mr. William Brown is another matter entirely."

"He lives next door," I said.

"Indeed," Edward agreed. "And he hates the fact that he shares a property boundary with Miss Zenobia Weekes and her Charm School for Exceptional Young Ladies. Not only does he make his feelings no secret, it can be difficult to pass before his house and not hear it."

That sounded familiar. I wondered if Linda Olson was a descendant or just someone who had bought the old man's house. Or perhaps the building had a strange energy that compelled its residents to accost passersby.

Now that I knew witches were really a thing, lots of other things I had thought impossible were becoming things I just had to start questioning.

Like aliens. Were they real, too?

"Can you introduce us?" Sophie asked.

"I can," Edward said, but there was something guarded in his tone.

"Is that a problem?" I asked. "We could probably just introduce ourselves—"

"Oh no, don't do that," Edward said. "He's very old-fashioned about that sort of thing. Young ladies, exceptional or otherwise, do not introduce themselves to men."

"Ugh," Sophie said, rolling her eyes.

"I'll just make the introductions, and once you get your feet under you, I'll hop over and call on Ivy," he said, looking wistfully at one of the upper windows of Coco's house.

Then we passed the charm school and the surprisingly sparse

hedges around Mrs. Olson's—I mean, Mr. Brown's—house until we reached the front walk.

Edward cleared his throat and adjusted his shirt and vest before ringing the bell. Just as the door started to swing open, he remembered his hat and whipped it off his head to thrust it behind his back. His hair whirled up, tried to follow the trajectory of his hat, then just collapsed in a tousle of waves over his forehead.

A perfect tousle of waves. He must have Sophie powers over his hair.

The man standing at the door was far too self-important to be a servant. He was looking at his pocket watch as opened the door as if even before we spoke, we were taking up entirely too much of his time. He was much taller than Mrs. Olson, with a full head of steely gray hair and a nose like a hatchet.

But the eyes. The eyes were the same. Just like Mrs. Olson's as she glared over the tops of her hedges. He didn't have to ask our business; that fierce glare did it for him. He tucked the pocket watch away, then planted a walking stick he had been holding tucked in his armpit between his feet and leaned most of his weight on it.

You'd think leaning on a walking stick would make him look infirm, harmless, but it didn't. It allowed him to loom over us like a villain in an old cartoon. The top of the cane was some sort of polished stone, gleaming gray with veins of white and black just visible between his bony fingers.

"Mr. William Brown," Edward said nervously. "You know me, I believe? Edward Scott?"

"I know you," Mr. Brown said, clearly wishing he didn't. "Why are you knocking at my door? I have no daughter for you to use to climb up in the world."

"Ah," Edward said, the old man's words clearly throwing him for a loop. I knew he hadn't yet introduced us, so I wasn't supposed to speak yet, but I couldn't keep my mouth shut.

"We're from next door," I said. "The school."

"Really?" he said with great disdain. "The charm school that completely fails in teaching any young lady even the rudiments of charm? Forward young ladies like yourself, for instance?"

"Miss Zenobia Weekes' school," Edward said, as if Mr. Brown might be thinking of some other place. "Forgive my manners. Ladies, may I present Mr. William Brown of Brown Lumber. Mr. Brown, this is Miss Amanda Clarke, Miss Sophie DuBois and Miss Brianna Collins, recently arrived from New Orleans."

I opened my mouth to correct the misconception that we were all from New Orleans, but Sophie reached behind Edward to dig her fingers into my arm, and I shut my mouth again.

Not important.

"That school," Mr. Brown said, "is a blight on this neighborhood. I've long said so—"

"Indeed, you have," Edward said, and I sensed he was running a frightful risk by interrupting the man, who responded by turning an alarming shade of purple. But Edward pressed on. "I'm sorry, Mr. Brown, but I'm wondering if you can tell us where you were yesterday evening? I think I might have seen you at the Hills' soiree."

"Yesterday evening?" Mr. Brown sputtered. "Yesterday evening I was in."

"All night?" Edward pressed.

"All night," Mr. Brown said darkly. "Not that it's anybody's business." Then he muttered under his breath, "why on earth I'd be at the Hills' soiree. I have no one left to marry off."

"So you were home all night?" I asked.

"Really, young lady," he said, offended, I think, that I was asking him any questions at all.

"It's just, we were wondering if you heard anything odd last night?"

"Odd, coming from your school?" he asked.

Sophie and I both nodded.

"Every sound that comes from that place is damned odd," he said, and I noticed he didn't apologize for cursing in front of us. We really weren't ladies in his eyes.

"Can you tell us more?" Sophie asked. "We just arrived, and we're really not sure what sort of place we've gotten mixed up in."

"No, I would say that you are not!" he boomed, but seemed to soften, as if pitying us poor travelers from afar. "Strange things happen there. Lights and sounds. Once I even thought it was on fire, and I could hear screams, but when I called the brigade, there was nothing. I don't appreciate being treated like a dotard," he added.

"No, I should say not," I said. I glanced over at Sophie and realized there was no one between us now. When had Edward taken off? Well, he had warned us.

"I would advise the three of you to pack up your things and head back to New Orleans at once," Mr. Brown said to us. "I won't spread rumors, no indeed I will not, but one hears the most frightful things about that place. No, I won't spread rumors, but I will tell you that anything you might hear, I am almost certain they are all true. Even the darkest, most ludicrous, diabolical tales that seem the ravings of a literary mind. Even those, I feel, do not scratch the surface of what really goes on inside those walls."

"Wow," I said. "Diabolical?"

"I shall not repeat rumors!" he said again. "But I will tell you this. Whatever goes on in that school, turning out fine young ladies is not its purpose. I've never seen a single refined lady emerge from Miss Zenobia's dubious tutelage."

"Mrs. Cynthia Thomas?" Sophie asked, and I braced for another blast of vitriol.

That didn't come.

"Mrs. Thomas is perhaps the exception," Mr. Brown allowed. "Although I prefer to think her family brought her up so well that even Miss Zenobia could not lead her wrong. Although why she still works with that spinster, I can't imagine. At least she is not a teacher."

"The reason we're asking if you heard anything odd last night," I said, sneaking a glance at Sophie to see if we were on the same page that now was the time to reveal our purpose. Sophie nodded, then jutted her chin up as if to give me courage. I looked back at Mr. Brown. "The reason why we're asking is that Mrs. Cynthia Thomas was murdered last night."

"Good lord!" Mr. Brown cried, clutching at his heart and staggering against the door frame. For a moment, I was genuinely afraid that he was having a heart attack and rushed forward to catch him. But he didn't fall. He did put a hand on my shoulder and use it to push himself back upright.

"I'm sorry," he said, stepping back from me. "That was a bit of a shock. Yes, a bit of a shock. You might have delivered that information in a gentler way."

"I'm sorry," I said. I couldn't find a diplomatic way to say that he seemed so lacking in empathy that nothing would bother him. I was half convinced he was only pretending to be so affected now.

Well, less than half.

"You're certain it was murder?" he asked. "She certainly appeared to be in fine health, but none of us are as young as we used to be."

"She was struck on the back of the head with something heavy," Sophie said. "We don't know what; the murderer hid it or took it with them."

"Horrible," Mr. Brown said. "I am truly sorry she died in such a way. A crime, yes, truly a crime on many levels. But why are you three asking me these questions? Shouldn't the police be the ones investigating?"

"You're absolutely correct," I said, then left that sentence hanging.

"Completely corrupt," he said. "I knew they were all on the dime, turning the other way when those fellows hop over to Minneapolis to rob banks, then hide out over here. Criminal! And turning the other way with all the bootlegging. Ridiculous! But not investigating the murder of a fine woman like Mrs. Cynthia Thomas. No, that's just not right."

"We're hoping if we find the guilty party, we can convince the police to step in," I said.

"That's noble of you, but completely unnecessary," he said, fidgeting with this pocket watch again. "I'll make some calls. Yes, I know people. I can put pressure on people. The police force will step up and do their jobs on this. They will, or my name's not William Brown."

Then, seeming to have forgotten we were even standing there on his front porch, he turned away and shut the door behind him.

"Well," I said as we walked back to the charm school's front porch. "That could be an interesting bunch of phone calls. He's going to have things to say to us the next time he sees us."

"Hey," Edward said, emerging from the shadows at the far end of the porch.

"Hey yourself," I said. "We thought you'd gone."

"No, I just went around back to talk to the folks in Mr. Brown's kitchen," Edward said.

"The servants?" I said. "Why?"

"I wanted to check his alibi," Edward said.

"What alibi?" Sophie said. "He said he was in all night. That doesn't rule out sneaking into our yard and killing Cynthia, then sneaking back into his own house."

"Usually not," Edward agreed, "but Mr. Brown is not a well man. And he's a widower with just one son, and he's away at Harvard. When he gets very ill, and apparently last night he was very ill, the housekeeper sits by his bedside all night long to tend to him."

"So someone was with him all night long?" I asked.

"Someone trustworthy?" Sophie asked.

"Oh yes," Edward said. "Mrs. Jones is the best. I've known her and her family forever. If she says she was with him all through the hours of the night while he was too ill to tend to himself, I believe her. I would stake my life on it."

"Then that's another suspect gone," I sighed.

"I don't suppose there's much point now, but we never asked him about the amulet," Brianna said, consulting her notes.

"No, he wouldn't know anything about it," I said.

"What amulet is this?" Edward asked. I looked at Sophie, and we seemed to agree without words how much we could say.

"It was a silver locket sort of thing that she always wore," I said.

"It wasn't on her body when we found it," Sophie added. "The murderer must have stolen it."

"So if you could find that amulet, you might be able to work your way back to finding the murderer?" he said.

"Maybe," I said, shooting Brianna a furious glance as she suddenly hopped up and down on her toes. Of course, she could do it with a spell, but she didn't need to say so out loud in front of Edward.

"Then I have one more person to introduce you to," Edward said, pushing up from where he had been sitting on the porch railing. "It's not in this part of town, but you'll be safe enough with me."

"Indeed," Brianna said, and the way the hand she held behind her back was brushing her skirt, I just knew she was holding that wand again.

"It's broad daylight," I added. "But just who are you taking us to see?"

"I have a friend, an old friend, who's in the trade," Edward said, his eyes suddenly as evasive as Brianna's.

"The trade?" Sophie repeated.

"Stolen goods. Mostly jewelry. Among other things," Edward said. "Point is, if anyone finds anything like that amulet, if they try to move it, Otto will know."

"What about Ivy?" I asked.

Edward glanced over his shoulder up at the hulking mansion behind him. "Ivy can wait," he said.

"Great," Sophie said, reaching out to take his arm one more time. "Let's go."

CHAPTER 18

$\mathcal{M}$iss Zenobia's Charm School for Exceptional Young Ladies was located almost at the very end of Summit Avenue, or perhaps it would be considered the beginning, in front of the steps of the cathedral. In 2018, the avenue took a turn past a little park before ending in Kellogg Boulevard, a road through the city that was bigger by far than even the highway that ran past my hometown.

In 1927, it was a little different. The buildings were lower, making the cathedral seem taller by comparison. The streets were the domain of a different sort of car, and the people passing on the sidewalks all looked overdressed in the warmth of the day to my eyes.

I felt overdressed myself, and desperate for a bottle of water. Something I was unlikely to find here. I met be able to procure a drink of water, but I doubted my body was going to cope well with 1927 water treatment standards.

If they even had any. I was suddenly finding all sorts of holes in my historical knowledge. But high school wasn't meant to prepare anyone for this sort of thing.

Edward led us away from the shops and restaurants, towards the warehouses and docks closer to the river. The people around us were changing, and our clothing was standing out more and more as we walked. Even Edward must have felt self-conscious, as he reached up to adjust his hat, changing its jaunty angle to something a bit more menacing.

I had taken a self-defense class in high school, but that had been a long time ago. I doubted I'd remember much if I needed it now beyond the basics of "kick them in the knee and run." Expecting Edward to defend all three of us was terribly unfair, but I didn't think it would come to that. Not with the surreptitious way both Brianna and Sophie were clutching their wands, hidden in the folds of their skirts.

I really wondered how Sophie was pulling that off, but then I remembered she had said her magic was based on feeling and hiding. I was starting to believe her on a deeper level.

Mostly, I was regretting my choice in shoes. The straps were going to make it tough to ditch them in a hurry, and I knew I'd never make it far running over these cobblestone roads with those heels.

Edward turned us down a short, narrow road that ran between two more populous ones. I would almost have called it an alley, but for the busy restaurant on one side, the crowd spilling out into the street, filling the space between the taller buildings with aggressive noise.

I didn't see any women in that restaurant.

"I should do the talking," Edward said to us in a low voice.

"He's your friend," I said.

"Yes, an old friend," he said in a way that left me feeling like I was missing part of his meaning.

"Are we in danger?" I asked.

"No, it's fine," he said, but I could see sweat trickling down his temples that hadn't been there before, and most of our walk had been in the shade.

"We're here if you need us," Sophie said. If he found that odd he didn't say so, just gave her a grateful nod then pressed on, past the crowd gathered around the open doors of the restaurant down into what really was an alley.

The stink of stale beer took me by surprise. Mr. Brown's talk of bootleggers had reminded me that we were in prohibition times.

Bathtub gin was one thing, but beer had been all but unobtainable.

But perhaps it was an old, lingering aroma because, in all honesty, it was almost completely overwhelmed by the smells coming from the piles of rotting vegetables and the miasma of urine flowing out of the darker corners.

"This had better be good," Sophie grumbled as she fell against me in her quest not to step in any of the puddles and ruin her lovely shoes.

Edward glanced back at us and briefly touched a finger to his lips, then waved for us to follow him down a narrow, steep flight of stairs into the darkness of a cellar under the restaurant.

Remember how I wasn't anxious to explore the cellar under Miss Zenobia's house? I was even less enthused about this one. But clearly, Sophie had no problems with cellars; she kept a firm grasp on my arm linked with hers as we ducked under cobweb-strewn beams.

The floor was sloped, scarred with the traces of past beer puddles that had long since run away over the many years the restaurant above had been serving customers who were looking for cheap food near the river. I wondered just how old it was. The building above wasn't particularly remarkable, but this basement felt old.

Hey, was I starting to feel things?

I looked over at Sophie, whose eyes were still fixed down as she stepped carefully. "What do you feel here?" I whispered.

"Old place," she whispered back. "Also, bigger than it looks. There's more to it. So much more. Like a cobweb that spread out under the whole city."

"Those caves Coco was talking about?" I wondered.

"Maybe," Sophie said. "Might be connected with the sewers as well."

"I definitely don't want to explore any of that," I said, and Sophie gave me a little smile of agreement.

Edward looked back at us and touched his finger to his lips again.

Sophie rolled her eyes, but I repeated his gesture and nodded in agreement.

Mostly I was thinking, the center of the web was where the spider lurked. And that was just where we were.

The top half of the room with the low beams had been largely open space, being directly under the restaurant with its apparently frequent spills. But the lower half of the room looked like a warehouse with crates stacked high against the walls and forming rows across the open floor. It seemed orderly as we passed down the center of the room, like library stacks on either side of us, but the more imaginative part of my brain had no problem creating an entire labyrinth twisting around us, luring us in, then interlocking behind us.

We'd never get out.

Then Edward stopped so suddenly that I collided with his back, then stumbled backward until Sophie caught me. The last row of crates reached nearly to the ceiling, creating a walled off space, the only narrow opening mostly blocked by Edward's wide shoulders. But I put a hand on his back for balance and rose up on tiptoes. I could see a man in a flat, shapeless cap leaning against a table. He appeared to be examining some object in his hands as three burly men stood in a row in front of him.

"It won't happen again, Otto," one of the men with his back to us said.

"Oh, I know it won't, Stevie," the man in the flat cap said, holding the thing in his hands up to the dim bulb that hung from a long line from the ceiling above. I still couldn't tell what he was holding.

Edward looked back over his shoulder at me, then pointedly at the hand I was resting on him, and I dropped back onto my heels, letting my hand drop away.

"You know what this is, right?" Otto asked. The others mumbled unintelligible answers. "Who knows?" Otto asked. "Stevie? No? Liam? Surely you know, Liam."

"It's a shillelagh," Liam said.

"Correct! It's a shillelagh. And what do you use a shillelagh for? Come on, any of you! Tommy. What does it look like it's for?"

I heard a sound, like something whistling through the air. Something heavy.

"Busting skulls, I'd reckon," Tommy said.

"Indeed, you are correct. Busting skulls. Now, do you fellows need to see this in action now, or will you trust me that I know my business?"

"You know your business," Liam said.

"Indeed, I do, Liam. Indeed, I do," Otto said, and the object whistled through the air again. "But busting skulls is not my business, is it, fellows? No, that's just… let's call it a hobby."

The men mumbled more words too low for me to catch. Then Otto stopped pacing back and forth, and his voice got lower, but still had the power to carry to my ears.

"Put some of the boys on watch," he said. "This won't happen again. It shouldn't have happened in the first place. What was the point of crafting this intricate organization if parts of you are going to forget that the other parts of you are out there? Use the boys. They're good workers."

"Yes, boss," the men said as one. Edward stepped back, making a bar of his arm to herd the three of us behind him as if he could hide us from the sight of the three ruffians. They each leered at us in turn, but not one of them lingered or spoke a word.

"Who's loitering outside my door now?" Otto demanded.

"Edward Scott," Edward said, barking his name out like he was at army roll call.

"Edward Scott?" Otto repeated. "Edward Scott doesn't show his face around these parts anymore, does he? I should check my whisper network."

"You should," Edward agreed. "And while you're at it, you can ask why it is no one has ever asked what a fine German fellow like yourself is doing trying to scare people with a shillelagh."

Otto laughed, a great booming laugh that echoed through the crate-made corridors around us.

"Get in here, you old dog," he said, and Edward stepped into the room. He glanced back and made the smallest of beckoning gestures for the three of us to follow him into the room.

This was clearly the inner sanctum, I realized as we stepped inside and I could finally see something outside of the patch of light the bulb threw on the table in the center of the room. There were smaller crates, the lids open to show the contents. Silver tea services, forks, knives, spoons, candlesticks. Entire jewelry boxes full of jewelry, as if some thief had taken the entire thing from someone's dresser without bothering to empty it of its contents.

And so many bottles of alcohol. I supposed it might be watered down, but it still had to be worth a fortune in this time.

"Edward, you've done well for yourself," Otto said, looking us over in a manner that was only a smidge less aggressive than the three men who had just left. I was starting to feel like I was going to need several showers when we got back home.

"They're not with me," Edward said. "I'm helping them with a thing. Otto, may I introduce Amanda Clarke, Sophie DuBois, and Brianna Collins. Ladies, this is an old schoolmate of mine, Otto Mayer."

"Schoolmates? Is that what we're calling it?" Otto asked, raising an eyebrow at Edward before crossing the room to bring Sophie's hand to his lips.

I couldn't help but notice he still had the shillelagh in his other hand. It was an ugly-looking weapon. No elegance, just bashing, and pain.

I flinched away from the sudden memory of the back of Cynthia's skull.

Had he done this? And now here we were, in the center of his web?

I think I was hyperventilating, or looking particularly pale maybe, but either way, Edward sensed my growing panic even as Sophie looked down her nose at the man in a shapeless, flat hat and grungy work clothes who was looking up at her as he pressed his lips to the back of her hand.

"There from Miss Zenobia's Charm School for Exceptional Young

Ladies," Edward said suddenly, too loudly. "New students," he added more softly.

"Really," Otto said, stepping back from Sophie. "Respect. All respect." He looked from Sophie—still mustering all the haughtiness she had inside of her, which was a lot—to me and then to Brianna, who to my surprise actually had her wand out. Had she panicked even more than I had?

"We need your help," Sophie said. "We're looking for an amulet and Edward here says you might be able to help us. Can you help us?"

"I'll do all I can," Otto said. "What does it look like?"

"I've drawn a picture," Brianna said, brandishing a page torn from her book. Otto took it from her and studied it carefully.

"No, I've not seen this. Gold?"

"Silver," Sophie said.

"No, I've definitely not seen it," Otto said, with what sounded like genuine regret. "I'll keep an eye out. More than that, I'll put the word out. If anyone anywhere on either side of the river tries to pawn something like this, if any of my boys even see someone walking around with something like this in their possession, I'll know about it."

"And?" Sophie prompted.

"I'll get word to Edward," he said. "Edward can get word to you, right?"

"We'll be in touch with Edward," Sophie said. "This is tremendously important," she added.

"Of course it is," Otto said, and despite the chill of the deep cellar, he appeared to have broken out in a fresh sweat. "Of course it is, if you're looking for it. I won't let you down."

"Thank you," I said, finally finding my voice. "We should be getting back."

"Of course," Edward said. "See you, Otto."

"Yeah, see ya," Otto said, still examining Brianna's drawing.

Once again, when we emerged back into the light of day, the sun seemed almost painfully bright.

"He changed his tune in a hurry," Sophie observed as we headed back towards Summit Avenue.

"You're new, so I don't suppose you know," Edward said. "The school has a bit of a reputation."

"We got a sense of that from Mr. Brown," I said.

"Oh, that's one thing," Edward said. "The society types have definite opinions, no question. But the other thing is, you never have to fear being robbed or bothered in any way. No one will ever put a finger on any of you or disturb that house in any way. Now that you've been seen by Otto, word will spread. Everyone will know who you are and where you live. You could walk through the docks at midnight on a moonless night, and no one will dare trouble you."

"I can't imagine why I'd want to do that," I said, "but thanks. It sounds like taking us to Otto accomplished a couple of things."

It was late afternoon by the time we were back on the front porch of the charm school, which still seemed as empty as ever.

"Thank you for all your help today," I said to Edward.

"Yes, it was nice meeting you," Sophie said, shaking his hand. Even Brianna almost looked him in the eye.

"It was no trouble, no trouble at all," Edward said, taking my hand last. He was about to release it when a sudden thought had him squeezing me tighter. "You'll be in touch? So we can pass information back and forth and such?"

"Of course," I said.

"Not that we need a reason to see each other again," he added, then seemed to realize he was still holding my hand.

It seemed a lot colder under that oak tree after he let me go. He slipped his hands into his pockets as if he felt it, too.

Then he looked up past the tree to the house next door. "I suppose," he said.

"Yes, Ivy," I agreed. "She's waited long enough."

He turned to head back down our front walk, but his eyes lingered on mine for an extra second or two, twinkling with a kind of mischief out of the corners, almost out of sight under the brim of his hat.

Then I ran to catch up with Brianna and Sophie as they strolled along the stepping stones to the back garden.

Time to go home.

CHAPTER 19

I didn't know about Brianna and Sophie, but having missed lunch and had nothing but coffee for breakfast I was starving by the time I blinked and found we were back in 2018. Mr. Trevor was standing in the solarium, staring out into the back garden, and gave us a happy wave as he saw us suddenly there.

"I suppose he was worried," I said. "We were gone most of the day, and it was our first trip."

"We should have worked out a way to contact that Tabitha person," Sophie said. "In case something happens, and we get stuck in the past."

"Yes, we should ask him," I agreed. Brianna didn't seem to hear us, trailing far behind as we followed the stepping stones around the side of the house to the front walk. She was turning pages in her little book and mumbling to herself. I couldn't hear the words, but the cadence sounded like she was questioning and answering herself.

"At last," Mr. Trevor said when he'd thrown open the front door to let us in. "I've made chicken and dumplings. It was meant for lunch, and while the soup keeps just fine, the dumplings were starting to get a bit dry."

"That sounds fantastic," I said. "I'm just going to run upstairs and change back to my normal clothes first."

"Me too," Sophie said, with a bit less enthusiasm.

Brianna said nothing, but she stayed trailing behind us until we reached the second floor. Sophie and I were nearly to the attic before we realized we had lost her.

"Library," Sophie guessed. "Just leave her for now. She's clearly working on something she needs to finish before we can properly talk to her."

"I'll bring her clothes down for her just in case," I said, carefully hanging my 1927 dress back in the closet, smoothing out the skirt so that it didn't wrinkle.

I had never gone to prom, and I had worn my only skirt under my graduation gown, one that had been my mother's before it was mine. If I let myself start going through that closet properly, to really think of those things as being mine, I don't know what would happen. It would be like one of those montages in a movie where the poor girl gets to shop to her heart's content; only it would take longer than an abbreviated cut from a pop song to process it all.

And I had a murder to solve.

When I was back in my normal clothes, I watched Sophie touch her hair, one quick stroke that had it all back in place. Then I gathered up Brianna's discarded things and the two of us headed down to the library.

Brianna was at the large table, dancing from one end to the other as she consulted a paragraph from this book, an illustration from another, always looking back to the little book in her hand and talking to herself. It wasn't so much her low volume that made it impossible for me to understand her. I had never heard anyone speak at such a speed before and in truncated sentences. Like she only needed to start a thought and then hop on halfway through to start the next one.

"I brought your clothes," I said, setting the bundle down on one of the chairs.

"Ah," Brianna said, and to my surprise, actually stopped her motion to look up from her book. Not at me, but at the clothes. "Thanks."

"You should eat with us," Sophie said. "Food for the brain. This will still be here when you're done."

"Unless you're at some crucial juncture?" I added.

Brianna bit down hard on her bottom lip, her brows drawing together in a scowl. Then that all dropped away, and she glanced up at us brightly.

"No, I can take a break," she said. "I'll just change and then follow you down."

I wasn't entirely convinced she wouldn't get sidetracked during that process, but Sophie and I left her and continued on to find Mr. Trevor filling bowls in the dining room. The light from the setting sun filtered in through the branches of the tree that loomed over that side of the house, making dappled patterns of gold all over the table and the back wall.

I glanced at the top of the hutch, but the box was not there. I wondered where Mr. Trevor had stored it, but decided that really it wasn't any of my business.

"This smells fantastic," I said instead, sliding into a chair and digging a spoon into my steaming bowl. I could smell the chicken, but also rosemary and thyme and the doughy smell of the steamed dumplings. "These aren't dry at all," I said around my first mouthful.

"You're kind to say so," Mr. Trevor said.

Sophie was looking down at her bowl with a strange look on her face, something like nostalgia but with a touch of a new realization.

"What is it?" I asked, again around a mouthful of food. I was really hungry.

"Nothing," Sophie said, filling her spoon with soup and putting it delicately in her mouth.

"You were thinking something," I said. "Like a memory, I think. Does this remind you of your mother's cooking or something?"

"Oh, no," Sophie said. "Quite the opposite. You know, I've been studying and training and devoting my life to dance and specifically ballet since I was, oh I guess, five years old."

"Wow," I said. I don't remember having any ambitions, in particular, when I was five. Getting home from kindergarten in time to watch Blue's Clues, maybe.

"That takes a lot of discipline," Mr. Trevor said. "And you were studying magic as well?"

"Less so," Sophie admitted. "But part of wanting to be a ballerina was strict control of my diet. That stew on the first day and the chili last night were marvelous, Mr. Trevor. And this is amazing as well. You're a tremendous cook."

"That wasn't always true," he admitted, but I could see him blushing at the compliment. "Miss Zenobia used to have a cook on staff when she still ran the school. I didn't learn how to cook until she needed me to take over. She was very forgiving of my first attempts. I think I've gotten the knack now, though."

"Yes," Sophie agreed. "It's total comfort food."

"Not what you're used to, I'm guessing," Mr. Trevor said. "You miss Louisiana food? New Orleans is one of the best places for cuisine in the world, but some of the less elaborate dishes should be things I could tackle if you like."

"No, this is perfect," Sophie said. "It's just, I've gone so long sort of mentally counting the cost of everything I eat, and just now I realized I don't have to do that anymore. Because I'm not going to be a dancer. I'm going to be a witch and a time portal guardian. So I guess I can eat what I like."

"Oh," I said. I'd pretty much always eaten what I liked. But I could appreciate that she was feeling a change. "That's why your face looked like that, then. You're kind of happy about it, but also kind of sad."

"Indeed," Sophie said. She used the side of her spoon to slice one of the plump dumplings in half, then spooned up half of it with a good measure of soup and put the whole thing in her mouth. The very opposite of dainty; she was eating like me now.

We smiled at each other across the table as we chewed.

"I think I've figured out a thing," Brianna said as she came in the doorway, little book still open in her hand. Mr. Trevor seemed to just know she wasn't going to look up and sprung out of his chair to guide her to the table and into a seat, moving the steaming bowl close enough to get even her attention.

"What have you figured out?" I asked.

"A thing about time," Brianna said. "That's sort of what my research was based on. I mean, not really. Really, I was studying the patterns and connections between magic as we use it and string theory, but part of that relates to time."

"Bree," Sophie said. "I think you're in danger of losing us very quickly."

Brianna glanced up as if startled to find us there. "Oh. Well, the thing is…" she trailed off again.

"String theory," I said, prompting her. "That's a physics thing." Which was the sum total I knew about string theory.

"You know how there are three dimensions of space and a fourth dimension of time?" Brianna asked.

Sophie and I nodded. We were with her so far.

"Well, in string theory, there are actually a bunch more dimensions than that," Brianna said.

And just like that, she lost us.

"Why don't you get super specific to the magic part of it?" I suggested.

"Okay," Brianna said, tapping the spine of the book against her lips as she pondered. "Well, what got me thinking was gravity. Gravity is the weakest of the four fundamental forces, and some theorize this is because it is spread across all of those little bundled up dimensions and not just the three plus one we see."

"Bundled up dimensions?" Sophie said.

"I should have said, those extra dimensions in string theory are really small. If you describe them mathematically, they look like this." She held her book open to us, showing a drawing that I was pretty sure could drive people insane, all twisting around itself over and over.

"Bree, can you make this simpler?" Sophie asked.

"Well, okay," Brianna said, flummoxed again. "Well, gravity spreads over extra dimensions, so anyway, I think the same thing might be true for magic."

"Okay," I said. If there was anything I knew less about than theoretical physics, it was magic.

"There are these things called branes," Brianna said. "They interact with each other. I won't try to explain. But they move in relation to each other. Theoretically." She glanced at my face, then at Sophie's, and bit her lip. "Some times magic is stronger than other times?" she ended feebly.

"That I can agree with," Sophie said. "I've been sort of meditating every day, just feeling the flow of magic. Some of that flow has patterns like the season or the time of day or the lunar cycle, but other parts ebb and flow in a way that just feels more random."

"Ooh, very good," Brianna said. "We should do some experiments together. You're way more sensitive than I am on this stuff."

"And you've learned all this from Miss Zenobia's library?" Mr. Trevor asked, sounding amazed.

"Well, not specifically. She didn't grasp it, but she was an excellent observer. If I had been here to explain it to her, I think she would have caught on at once."

"What does this mean for us?" I asked.

"Oh yes," Brianna said, consulting her book again. "I thought that Miss Zenobia appearing at the full moon was just a lunar cycle thing. Very common with witches since the dawn of witches, really. But she had a subtler sense of things. She missed a full moon between when she passed and when we were summoned, didn't she?"

"She did," Mr. Trevor agreed.

"Yes, she knew this would be a better time with a stronger total flow of magic. Otherwise, her spell would have had a much smaller effect."

"That's interesting, but how is it significant now?" I asked.

"The murder happened very close to the same point," Brianna said. "The obvious sign of the lunar cycle isn't the stronger part of the magic flow. It's the invisible part involving the extra dimensions. But that's ebbing now too."

"Is it going to be harder to get into the past now?" Sophie asked.

"Not for us," Brianna said. "But for whoever has the amulet. Think about it: whoever killed Cynthia carried her body to 2018 and left her here, then went back to 1927. But that amulet wasn't designed for a person lugging another person. It only happened because of the timing of it all. And I'd guarantee whoever has the amulet now doesn't know that."

"So what do we do?" I asked. "We don't know who has it or how much they know."

"We'll find them, if we keep investigating," Sophie said with a confidence I didn't feel.

"In the meantime," Brianna said and discovered the bowl of food in front of her for the first time. She put a spoonful in her mouth and seemed to melt in her seat with a warm yummy noise, rolling her eyes back in sheer bliss.

"In the meantime?" I prompted.

"In the meantime, I can put a spell on the portal itself. I'll know when the amulet passes through, like an intruder alarm."

"Oh, brilliant," Sophie said, and Brianna beamed.

"I'm afraid that won't work," Mr. Trevor said regretfully.

"What do you mean? Why wouldn't it? The theory is sound, and I'm a pretty good witch," Brianna said.

"Yes, but Miss Zenobia was a very powerful witch with centuries more of experience than you," Mr. Trevor said. "Like normal people, most witches are good. But a few aren't, and Miss Zenobia was always a tempting target for their machinations. She was worried about other witches sensing Cynthia moving back and forth through time on an almost daily basis. That amulet was crafted just for her, not just to carry her across time, but to hide her from other witches. Any spell you can think of, Miss Zenobia surely thought of it first and put a countering spell on the amulet."

Brianna slumped in her chair, spoon dripping over her placemat.

"We'll find it," I said to her. "We'll find that amulet the old-fashioned way. And then it will be yours to study. Just think of all you're going to learn from it."

Brianna didn't quite return to the manic state she had been in when she'd come into the dining room, but she was at least recovered well enough to finish eating.

I just wished I really believed we could find that amulet. It was tricky enough when we didn't know it was capable of actively evading our detection.

Or at least Brianna's and Sophie's detection. All I had to go one was my own two eyes, and they were feeling woefully inadequate these days.

CHAPTER 20

For a good chunk of my junior high school years, my mother and I lived next door to a couple prone to very loud, very frequent disputes. They would start about the time I was getting ready for bed and would stretch on until the wee hours of the morning.

Honestly, I don't know what the point of it was. Either you get along, or you don't, and if you don't, then you shouldn't be sharing a tiny box of an apartment.

That might be a bit simplistic. But I was thirteen. Lots of things were more black and white then.

At any rate, the only defense I had against this nightly invasion of chaos was my Walkman. It didn't even play CDs; it played cassettes, which were really hard to come by. I listened to the same three The Cure albums over and over until that loud couple finally moved out.

I'm not even sure they broke up. I think they moved out still together.

But whatever, the point is, falling asleep to music was something that had once been normal for me. So I only had that one sleepless night due to the jazz music. By the third night, it was almost a comfort. I went to bed with my head spinning from the lack of clear-cut suspects in our investigation and a lot of confusing dinner talk about string theory and branes. Then the sounds of a trumpet carried through my closed window, each note clear and sweet, and I was soon fast asleep.

In the morning, I put on the last of my clean clothes. I had only packed enough for a weekend, and here it was Monday morning. I was going to have to figure out where the washing machine was. Probably in that cellar that didn't connect to the house.

Ugh, that was going to suck in January.

At some point, I was going to have to go back to Iowa to get the rest of my things and to tell the Schneidermans that I wouldn't be coming back. I pushed that thought aside. That was going to be so hard to do; I just couldn't think about it now.

I went down the back stairs, pausing on the second floor to listen until I made out the voices of both Brianna and Sophie, up before me and already working together in the library.

In high school, my best friend Christine had a boyfriend, but I didn't. Hanging out with the two of them had never felt as third wheel-y as I felt in that moment on the stairs.

I went the rest of the way down to the kitchen and saw to my surprise there was no coffee waiting for me in the machine. Had Mr. Trevor slept in, or forgotten about us before his morning walk?

Well, it's not like I didn't have years of experience making large quantities of coffee.

I started opening cabinet doors in search of the coffee and coffee filters, and the thought of going back to Iowa floated back up to the fore of my mind.

I didn't necessarily have to tell the Schneidermans I wasn't coming back. I didn't necessarily have to bring all of my stuff to Minnesota. If the last couple of days had proven anything, it was that Sophie and Brianna didn't need me for anything they couldn't do themselves. It might take three witches to guard the portal, but if that was the case, it should be three actual witches, not two witches plus a girl who could make the coffee.

A girl who could make the coffee when Mr. Trevor forgot, I amended and felt very low indeed.

I heard a scamper of footsteps coming down the hall and was just musing that it had to be Brianna because no dancer would tromp down a hall like that when a bright bolt like electric fire shot past my head, exploding a plant hanging near the window behind me.

Coffee grounds flew up into the air as I ducked behind the counter and started crawling towards the back door. I was nearly there when I saw a pair of ankle boots slide in front of my crawling hands, blocking my way.

I scrambled back and away just before another bolt of light crackled and exploded, leaving a black, smoking hole in the tile. I crawled as quickly as I could towards the butler's pantry, but the image of Brianna standing over me, wand raised as her other hand pointed to me with three fingers and her mouth whispered words of power, was seared on my brain.

What was going on? Was she possessed?

One thing was certain: she was definitely trying to kill me.

I got to my feet once I was in the pantry and started grabbing everything my hands could find on the counters, flinging silver teapots and serving trays and napkin rings back into the kitchen.

Something hit her; I heard her say, "oof" as something clanged. But it wasn't enough to stop the next blast of energy exploding the cabinet full of china behind me.

And now I was bleeding everywhere, from a million tiny cuts, and the floor was covered in slivers of the finest bone china.

"Sophie!" I yelled, pulling myself into the hallway to run towards the front door. "Help!" I pulled all the dining room chairs over as I ran past them. It wouldn't slow Brianna down much, but it was better than nothing.

The extent of my plan was to reach the front door and get outside. I was pretty sure that Brianna wouldn't do magic where everyone could see. At least I hoped she wouldn't.

But just as I was reaching the foyer, Sophie stepped down from the bottom of the stairs.

"Thank goodness!" I said, skidding to a halt. "Brianna has gone crazy. What were you two digging into upstairs? Mr. Trevor said a lot of that stuff was really dangerous—"

But there was something cold in Sophie's eyes, something that made me realize she wasn't on my side either.

Then she lifted up in a dancer's pose, swinging her arms around then extending her fingers towards me.

And, just as if she had summoned a hurricane wind, I was blown off my feet, sliding on my back down the hardwood floor of the hallway.

I only stopped when the top of my head hit Brianna's feet. She bent at the waist to look down at me, her hair falling around both of our faces as if to create a tunnel between us.

Then she raised that wand again, and I threw myself back into motion.

I didn't know any magic, and I had never studied any dancing. But I had spent a lot of time in weight rooms when I played hockey, and I had learned lots of little things from the other gym rats. One of them was a little move called a kip up. You've seen it in movies. It's how the likes of Bruce Lee get up off the ground.

I hadn't done one in years. But adrenaline is an amazing drug.

I threw my weight back onto my hands, and Brianna shrieked and stumbled back away from me. I wasn't really trying to kick her, but it probably looked that way from where she was standing.

Then I kicked my legs out and flipped myself up onto my feet, hands up and ready for whatever Sophie was going to throw at me next.

But there was no reason to wait for her to do her thing. She cast spells like the benders in that M. Night Shyamalan movie. Way too slowly.

She swept her arms back, and I could feel the beginnings of that wind pulling at the curls of my hair.

But the moment her arms were back, I charged her, wrapping my arms around her and throwing her back into Brianna.

She hadn't eaten enough of Mr. Trevor's cooking to weigh more than a feather yet. But when I threw her back into Brianna, they both went down in a tangle of arms and legs.

Nets don't weigh much either, but they sure can slow you down.

I started for the door again, but even still tangled up with Sophie Brianna was capable of throwing another bolt that exploded over the doorknob, crackling like fire over the brass.

I turned and ran for the stairs. It felt really hopeless. There was nowhere I could hide, nothing I could do to fight them. But I would buy every minute I could. Because every minute that passed was another chance for something to change.

Not that I was planning to wait for a rescue. Who would possibly turn up to rescue me from two rogue, possibly possessed witches?

No, I was on my own. And I needed a weapon. A weapon that would fight witches.

Hysterical laughter started to bubble up inside of me, but I swallowed it back down as I charged up the stairs to the second floor.

My only chance was Miss Zenobia's office. It was stuffed with strange objects. There had to be something in there that would even the odds.

CHAPTER 21

I ran into Miss Zenobia's office and slammed the door shut. Then I shut the locks and bolts, one after the other. There were more locks on that door than on the door of a New York apartment.

I tried not to dwell on why that might be. The locks were on this side, so this was the safe side. That thought gave me enough comfort.

After I slid the last bolt home, I spun around to take inventory of the room around me. Fire poker, that was a mundane start. I grasped it in my hand, then got back to my frantic search.

The truth was, lots of things looked like weapons. There was a glass ball on the mantlepiece that appeared to be filled with small golden disks with razor-sharp edges. Less a fortune teller's crystal ball than a really pretty shrapnel grenade. And as I looked, those disks were moving around inside the ball, anxious to get out and start bouncing around the room. I'd be cut up as well as the other two, and I was already bleeding all over from the china cabinet explosion.

So that would be a last resort.

I turned my attention to the desk as the first energy bolt hit the door like a crackling battering ram. The hinges shrieked in protest.

It wasn't going to matter how many locks there were if Brianna just blew a hole in the entire wall.

And who was going to pay for the damages? We were housemates now. We had to have a house meeting and come up with a written agreement on such things, clearly.

Yeah, so that was the second bubble of hysterical laughter I had to swallow back down. But I was way out of my element. Hysteria was all I had left.

I looked down at the floor next to the desk. There was a wire basket next to the desk. A wastepaper basket, and yet the paper inside the basket didn't look like it was waste. It was lovely, glossy and multi-colored, and it looked like it had all been carefully folded before being dropped in the basket.

Not wadded up, folded. Like origami.

The second bolt hit the door, hard enough to make the whole house shudder. There was a moment of silence, then the door gave a creaking groan and fell flat on the floor like a drunk passing out at a party.

"Come on, you guys," I said, keeping the poker tucked behind me and backing up until I felt the top of the basket pressed against my calf. "What's going on here? This is crazy."

Brianna didn't say anything, just stepped over the smoking wood of the door to stand by the fireplace. Sophie came in behind her, stepping to the other side of the room.

"If you want me to leave, I'll just go," I said. "I don't want to be here. It's totally understandable that you don't want me here. You don't have to kill me!"

Brianna had been raising her wand again. I saw her hesitate for just a moment, but Sophie raised her chin and Brianna stiffened both her body and her resolve. Her other hand stretched out to me, those three fingers pointing to the center of my chest. Perhaps that was how she took aim. I didn't know a thing about magic.

I raised the fire poker like a sword, and while she was looking at the end of that, I reached back and grasped the basket. Then I fell back on one knee and tossed the contents of the basket high into the sky.

The little bits of paper screeched. Even before they stretched out their crumpled wings and took to the air, they screeched.

But in a moment they were everywhere, flapping in a glittering array of colors, swarming like rabid butterflies over Sophie and Brianna.

Brianna cried out and threw her arms over her head. I would swear the little paper cranes were pecking at her with the small folds of paper that were their beaks.

Sophie spun in a circle, bringing that hurricane force wind in a tight cyclone around her. The cranes were caught up in it, but so was what appeared to be a decorative bowl full of acorns. It was only when the acorns started to explode like the flak bursts from an anti-aircraft gun that I realized they were, of course, not merely decorative.

I knew I couldn't hide in Miss Zenobia's office. It wasn't big enough, and when Brianna's attempt at using her wand to rid herself of the paper birds set the rug in the corner on fire, it certainly wasn't safe. I jumped over the length of the door, landing in the hallway, then running back down the hall.

"The door!" Sophie yelled.

"Hold on!" Brianna shrieked, then that shriek ratcheted up to one of pain.

I abandoned my dash for the back door, diving into the library instead. I ran to the back of the room, furthest from the windows, and dove under a table. Not the large table that Brianna spent all of her time at, but a smaller one tucked away in what I could only hope was a forgotten corner.

I put my hands over my mouth and tried to slow my breathing.

It took a long time. Not only was I terrified, I was beginning to realize I wasn't in the best of shape. I had missed too many workouts since high school.

Actually, I couldn't remember the last time I'd made it to the gym. Working on my feet all day in the diner was so draining. I was regretting letting that get to me now.

But it was too late. I could hear footsteps. Brianna's were the louder ones coming from the front of the library, and she was breathing nearly as hard as I.

But I also heard Sophie's softer steps coming from the back door to the library. Her breathing was light and controlled.

I put a knuckle in my mouth and bit down hard, keeping my breath as quiet as possible.

But really, it had always just been a matter of time. Sophie's feet stopped at the end of my row. I tucked into a tighter ball and held my breath. Then Brianna's feet joined hers.

I waited for them to start walking towards me, but the feet stayed where they were for a long time. I wondered if they were mouthing words to each other and communicating in some special to witches kind of way.

Then there was a swish, a sound I was getting all too familiar with: Brianna's wand through the air as she raised it high. I could imagine those three fingers of her other hand pointing to where I hid under the table.

Then the table was gone, lifted up into the air. It sailed between Sophie and Brianna to land with a crash behind them.

I only had one thought left in my head. Just one, but every fiber of my being wanted to hear it answered.

"Why?" I shrieked.

I wanted an answer, but I didn't really expect to get one. I wrapped my arms around my head like they taught us in grade school for tornado drills.

The Schneidermans were going to wonder what happened when I never came back.

Just the two of them. That was pretty much it. Perhaps a regular or two might be curious. But no one was really going to miss me.

"I was really hoping this would work," Brianna said, sounding confused.

"It was worth a shot," Sophie said. "But clearly, yeah, it didn't work."

I pulled my arms down enough to peer past my elbow to the two of them standing at the end of the row. Brianna's wand was nowhere in sight, and she looked deeply distressed. Like she'd just flunked in math class.

"What didn't work?" I asked, still not ready to untuck my body. This could be a trick.

"Magical gifts have been known to manifest under stress," Sophie said.

"Did yours?" I shot back. I felt a teensy bit bad when she flinched, then reminded myself that she had just tried to kill me. Or make me think she wanted to kill me. Same difference.

"No," she admitted. "My mother spent years working on my sensing of magic, and the hiding thing I worked out on my own. The wind thing I did by mistake at a dance recital once when I got all caught up in the emotion. That was an interesting night."

"My mentors taught me a lot of little things first," Brianna said. "Making knots untie and spoiling milk and things like that."

"And that energy bolt thing?" I asked.

"It's the only offensive thing I know," she said. "I read it in a book and worked out how to do it. Mostly, I stick to smaller spells. The kind that encourage people not to notice me."

"And why couldn't I start with the sensing or the small stuff?" I asked.

Now they both looked miserable, but I wasn't going to let my glare up until one of them answered.

"I..." Brianna started, then glanced over at Sophie. "We felt like maybe a faster course was required."

"Because of the calling to guard the portal," I said.

"Not just that it was necessary," Sophie said, risking taking a step closer to me. "We felt like, because you're so much older than we were when we started, that a faster path would be easier. Better. Something you could do."

"Well," I said, getting to my feet and brushing myself off. How did the floor of a library get so dirty? "You were right. It didn't work."

"We're really sorry," Brianna said. "We won't try it again."

"Or throwing me in the river, or whatever other ridiculous things are in these books?" I persisted.

"That wouldn't be in *these* books," Brianna said. "These are proper magic books, not anti-witch propaganda."

"We won't," Sophie promised.

"Okay," I said. "Just to be clear. I'm open to any kind of test or lesson or whatever. I'd love to be able to access the power you two have, and if Miss Zenobia thought I had it too, it's worth following up on, right? But we're going to talk about it first. What you want to do and what it entails. No more surprises. No more ambushes."

"No more," Sophie agreed, then rubbed at her tailbone. "I don't think I could even do it again."

"Sorry," I said. "You did trigger a fight-or-flight response in me. Just not the fight you were looking for."

"We'll find it," Brianna said. "I know we will."

I nodded, then brushed past them to go back down to the kitchen, clean up the spilled grounds, and start the process of making coffee all over again.

Just as I was passing between them, they both looked at me. Just darting glances, but it was enough. Despite their words of encouragement to me and to each other, they were both disappointed that I hadn't manifested my power.

If that panic and terror hadn't triggered it, what would?

Oh, how I really didn't want to know.

CHAPTER 22

$\mathcal{B}$rianna might focus on spells to help people ignore her, but she knew a few others as well. By the time I had the coffeemaker all sorted and was leaning back against the opposite counter to watch the drops fall into the carafe, she had cleaned up every bit of damage. The china, intact once more without so much as a seam to show where it had broken, was stacked neatly in the cabinet. The chairs in the dining room and library were all in their proper positions, as was the table.

I'm not sure if she could fix what happened in Miss Zenobia's office, but she got the door back up into the frame, and everything looked normal.

Sophie joined me at the counter, watching the coffee drip. Then Brianna came to lean on the other side of me. None of us said a word. I think we were all really tired.

It had been an exhausting day, and it wasn't quite seven.

Something rapped loudly, and I jumped, spinning around to see Nick tapping at the kitchen window. His eyes widened at my reaction, and he mouthed that he was sorry, then pointed around to the back of the house.

"I hope he has some news," Sophie said as I went to open the back door to let him in. I hoped so too. More information on the murder weapon would be nice.

"Good morning," Nick said when I had opened the door. He stepped carefully over the police tape and climbed up onto the porch. "I was just walking the dog when I got a call from Nelson, and I told him I'd bring you all up to date. Is Mr. Trevor in?"

We all looked at each other. We weren't sure where he was when he was inside the house, let alone when he was outside.

Nick waved off the question as unimportant before any of us had even worked up an answer. "No worries. Nelson asked you all to stay in town until you were cleared, and that's happened now. I know it's Monday morning, and you were all only here for the weekend, so I thought I'd come over to see if you were up so I could let you know. Early risers like me, I see."

"Actually, we'll be staying longer," I said.

"Oh, yeah?"

"The three of us inherited the school, so we'll be living here," I told him. "Coffee?"

"Yeah, coffee would be great," Nick said. "Black is fine." There was a smile that really wanted to erupt across his face, but he kept wrestling it back down.

Sophie had already poured out three cups of coffee. She pushed two of them towards me, then turned to get another mug for herself. I put a dollop of butter in mine, then handed the other to Nick.

"Thanks," he said. "Wow. That's good. What kind is it?"

"I actually have no idea," I said. "Mr. Trevor buys it, and it's in an unmarked canister. I'll ask him the next time I see him."

"He must get it local," Sophie added.

"Did Nelson tell you anything else that you can share?" I asked. "They know for sure she wasn't killed here?"

"Yes, that's clear from the crime scene," he said. "And you can pull that tape down if you want. They aren't going to need to look at it again."

"Good to know. Thanks." It would make getting to the backyard while dressed for the 1920s easier if we could just use the back door.

"The bad news is that it's very unlikely they'll be able to solve the case," Nick said gravely.

"Because this wasn't the scene of the crime," I guessed.

"Right. No suspects, no sign of a murder weapon. Unless someone stumbles upon the primary crime scene, or unless—heaven forbid—this was a random thing, and the killer strikes again, they just don't have enough to go on. And with their caseload, they can't spend hours following up unlikely leads."

"It's a shame, but we understand," Sophie said.

"I wish we could do more," Nick said.

"We?" I said, teasing. His cheeks flushed, and he bent his head to take another sip of coffee. "Well, you'll be police soon enough. I shouldn't make fun."

"But you're right, though. I'm still a lot of steps away," he said.

"They didn't find the murder weapon," Brianna said.

"No, they did not," Nick confirmed. "Blunt force trauma. They know that much."

"Like a rock?" I asked.

"No, not like a rock," Nick said. "Narrower and longer. But short, not like a baseball bat. And probably heavy. It only took one blow."

"Heavy, or the murderer was strong," Sophie said, and I could see the gears of her brain turning. Mine were turning too.

"Er, yes," Nick said, flustered. Perhaps he thought we were unnecessarily morbid. Then he swallowed the last of his coffee. "I hate to run, but I do have to go. Classes start today."

"You should have said so," I said, walking with him to the back door. "We wouldn't have detained you if we knew."

"You didn't detain me. I had plenty of time," he said. I saw Sophie and Brianna exchange a smiling glance but ignored it as we passed into the solarium and I held the door for him.

"I'm glad you're not leaving," he said.

"Me too," I said, surprised to find that it was true.

"Even better, I'll be your next-door neighbor now," he said.

"Really?" I asked. For some reason, a vision of Linda Olson flew through my mind. She would be a tough one to live with.

"Yeah," Nick said. "I've been bunking with some friends from high school who live over a bar downtown, and that's been fun, but my grandfather needs more help than I can give him from that distance, so I'm moving in with him."

"Cool," I said.

"Yeah?" he asked, his eyes searching my face, for what I wasn't sure.

"Yeah, very cool," I said. "Stop over for coffee anytime. We always have tons."

"I will," he said. He lingered for a moment, but just before it got really awkward, he stepped back out onto the porch. He bent to catch the end of the police tape and followed the length of it, bunching it up into a big yellow ball. He ended at the corner of the house and raised the sticky wad in one last salute before disappearing into the side yard.

"Someone's made a friend already," Sophie said as I came back into the kitchen.

"We're all friends," I said, heading to the coffee machine for a refill. I wasn't going to make it through the day without a lot more caffeine.

"Well, there's friends, and then there's *friends*," Sophie said, kicking her accent up to full Creole. Brianna just grinned at me, and I felt my cheeks heating.

"What he said about the murder weapon," I said hurriedly, and slid into my chair at the table.

That sobered them up at once.

"Long, narrow, heavy," Sophie agreed. "Like that shillelagh."

"Are we suspecting Otto?" Brianna asked.

"You don't think he seems prone to violence?" Sophie asked.

"Well," Brianna said, twisting her hands together.

"I think I know what Brianna means," I said. "Otto has definitely cracked some skulls with that club before. But only in, like, gang fights. Turf wars, teaching his own underlings a lesson, maybe. But not old women. Not Cynthia."

"So he's a thief with a code," Sophie said skeptically.

"Thief, bootlegger, goodness knows what else," I said. "But yes. I think he has a code."

"I'm not so sure," Sophie said, eyes narrowing as she assessed me. "I think you think so because he's Edward's friend, and you're taken with Edward."

I nearly choked on my coffee. "Taken with Edward?"

"I thought so too," Brianna said.

"Weren't you just implying that about Nick?" I asked.

"Yeah, we totally were," Sophie said, and an evil grin played across her lips.

"Anyway," I said, trying to get back on topic. "I have another reason for doubting it's Otto."

"A real one?" Sophie teased.

"Fear," I said. "You saw how he changed when he knew we were part of the charm school. Everyone knew Cynthia worked for Miss Zenobia. Edward said no one in 1927 would touch us, and based on how Otto reacted, I think that's true."

"I do too," Sophie conceded. "So our suspect either didn't know Cynthia was part of the school—"

"Which seems unlikely since she was murdered in the backyard there," I interrupted.

"Not necessarily true," Brianna interrupted. "You're assuming she was killed and pushed through the time portal, but it's just as likely she was murdered somewhere else, carried to the house, and then pushed through the portal."

"That means the murderer didn't push her through the portal by accident," I said. "They knew it was there."

"Which brings us back to the 'why haven't they tried to use the amulet yet?' question," Sophie said.

We all lapsed into silent regard of our coffee for a long moment.

"What else were you going to say?" I asked at last.

"Hmm?" Sophie said, still mostly regarding her coffee.

"Either the murderer didn't know Cynthia was part of the school or..." I prompted.

"Oh," Sophie said. "They didn't know, or they didn't care. They weren't afraid of Miss Zenobia."

"Who wouldn't be afraid of Miss Zenobia?" Brianna asked in a whisper. "Even if you didn't know she was a witch, she was fearsome. That glower. She had an energy. I bet her students were in terror of her."

"Not all of them," I said. "She was putting all the energy to bear on us to get us to swear. And Cynthia, for one, really seemed to love her."

We lapsed into another thoughtful silence.

"So if we don't think it was Otto," Brianna said after some time. "Who else could it be?"

"We didn't exhaust Coco's list of possible suspects," Sophie said. "Some were clearly ridiculous, but others might not be. In prohibition, it was really easy to get tangled up in the mob because they had their fingers in so many pies. What if someone was trying to get protection money from Miss Zenobia?"

"I think that someone would be dead," I said. "But there is another thing. Mr. Brown's cane."

"Long and narrow," Sophie agreed. "But the heavy bit at the top was awfully round."

"We don't have the actual autopsy report," I pointed out. "We have a summary of a summary."

"Still, he had an alibi too, right?" Sophie said.

"That's two degrees away from actual proof, too," Brianna said. "We have to trust that Edward is right about the housekeeper and that the housekeeper watched as diligently as she said she did. If the murder happened at three to five in the morning, was she still as alert as she thought she was after being up all night tending to a sick man?"

"We'd also have to question her being right about how sick he was," I added. "A sick man couldn't hit that hard."

"Not a physically sick one," Sophie agreed.

I sighed. "We might not be able to solve this."

"Hey," Sophie said, catching my hand and squeezing it. "Remember, Cynthia believed in you. She believed in all of us. She didn't know this was going to happen to her, but I'm sure if she did, she'd trust in us to bring her killer to justice."

"We just need to work a little harder," Brianna said.

"We need more clues," I said. "And all the clues are in the past. And we didn't find them when we were there before. Now it's been days since the murder. I doubt there's anything left to find."

"It depends on where the primary crime scene was," Brianna said. "If it was somewhere remote, it could still be untouched. We just have to have a little hope."

"Hope," I repeated. I doubted I could muster much of that. "What we need is a plan."

"I need to do some research," Brianna said. Clearly, that was her answer to everything.

"I'm going to do some exercises," Sophie said. "Sometimes that helps me think. Maybe I'll come up with something good." Her little shrug was as dejected as I felt.

"What about you, Amanda?" Brianna asked.

"Me? I guess I'll just go for another walk."

"That helps you think?" Sophie asked.

"I guess so," I said.

In truth, I had never had a pressing need to think about much of anything before. I had lived a pretty boring life up until a few days ago.

I reached out with my senses, trying to feel that old compulsion that told me what to do. It had told me when to stay home, when to go into work early, to never, ever leave my hometown until Cynthia came to find me there.

But it was silent now. I was on my own. And I was so unprepared.

CHAPTER 23

 got about five blocks away from the house before the rain
started. There was no warning feeling of mistiness to the
air, no occasional drops building in frequency. No, it was like the sky
above me just opened up and dumped everything.

I ran back to the house, but not fast enough. By the time I got
there, I was soaked to the skin. And I had nothing clean to change
into.

Or at least, no clean, modern clothes to change into. Not having a
lot of other options, and no idea where to find Mr. Trevor, I tromped
up the stairs, first to the bathroom on the third floor to get a towel for
my dripping hair, then up to the attic.

As I climbed the last few steps, I heard sounds coming from the
attic, a soft swoosh and tap, swoosh and tap. I crept up to the doorway
to see Sophie spinning down the length of the room. One complete
spin, stopped by a touch of her toe, then another spin and stop, the
entire movement tracing a long oval around the room.

She had pushed the various chests and boxes up against the walls
where the sloping ceiling was too low for her to dance under. But she
hadn't taken a broom to the dusty floor; I could see the places where

her slippered feet had disturbed the gray accumulation of decades of neglect.

I watched her spin to the very back of the house, not quite brushing against the cupboard doors, then start spinning back on the side of the room opposite the door. Her eyes were closed, and her arms were trying out different arrangements. Something told me she was practicing not dance but magic, reaching out with her senses and moving her arms, hands, and fingers through the invisible forces she could feel flowing around her.

I didn't want to disturb her, but I was getting cold in my wet clothes, so as quietly as I could, I crept along the length of the room to the cupboards. I gently eased one of the doors opened and grabbed whatever came first to hand, then scurried back to the door and down the stairs to my bedroom.

I had grabbed what looked to be the sort of dress a farmer's wife would wear, sturdy and built for work. I hadn't taken any underwear or shoes, but that wouldn't matter.

I left my own things draped over furniture to dry, then headed downstairs to see what Brianna was up to.

Brianna was in full mumbling to herself mode, moving from book to book, turning pages and occasionally jotting something down in her own notebook. Not the little one she carried in her pocket, but a large tome with cream-colored pages, unlined and full of as many illustrations as writing.

I'm guessing the illustrations were more of her string theory drawings because none of it looked like anything to me.

Clearly, she was just as engrossed as Sophie, if not more so, and I didn't want to disturb her either. Still, every so often in her hunt for this bit of information or that she would pick up one of the half-dozen or so teacups that were scattered across the table among and even on the books. Each cup proved empty when she tried to drink from it, and she set them back down and promptly forgot them.

Well, making Brianna more tea was one contribution I could make. I went down to the kitchen.

While waiting for the kettle to boil, I dug through the butler's pantry until I found a little bamboo tray just large enough for tea for one. In one of the cupboards was an array of those little teapots that sit atop matching cups. I grabbed one that was covered with owls with large, wise eyes and brought it and the tray back into the kitchen.

I grabbed the sugar bowl to add it to the tray, but it felt light in my hand. I lifted the lid and gave the bowl a little shake, but it was quite empty.

Where would Mr. Trevor keep the rest of the sugar? Or was he hoarding it like the maid at the Thomas house that was driving Helen crazy? What was her name? Molly?

I saw a row of canisters on the top shelf of one of the cabinets, too high even for me to reach, and I had to pull over a chair.

It was at about that point that I started to feel the déjà vu. It got stronger as I took the canister down from the shelf and, still standing on the chair, looked inside.

You could hide anything inside a canister of sugar if you buried it deep enough. Was anyone going to give it more than a cursory glance?

I don't know how long I stood on that chair staring down into the canister of sugar. The déjà vu feeling was so strong it was like I was outside of myself, watching myself slowly step down from the chair and sit on it, still looking down at the sugar.

I had never met Molly, the maid Helen had so distrusted. I wasn't sure what motive she could possibly have. By Helen's own account, she had been an admirer of Cynthia's, and Cynthia had been lending her books and encouraging her to pursue her own education.

But I should have at least met her, asked her a few questions.

Like, how long had she worked for the Thomases? Was she aware of what Cynthia did every day? Did she have a clue what the amulet did?

Had she taken it and hidden it deep inside the sugar, then put the canister up high? She must have been about to be caught with her mistress's jewelry and only had a moment to act.

Then the déjà vu feeling faded, and I took a deep breath. I was no longer feeling like every present moment was a memory I was just remembering, which was a relief. Really, déjà vu that lasted longer than a flash was quite unsettling.

I put the chair away and was just spooning tea into the basket inside the pot when quite a different feeling came over me.

I had to go back to 1927. I knew it; it was a surety. I was compelled.

I knew this feeling, this compulsion well, but never like this. Never suddenly dawning in the middle of a day. It had always been a feeling I woke up with before. What did this change mean?

Perhaps later I could talk to Brianna and Sophie about it. Maybe it was a magic thing, but maybe it wasn't. In the meantime, the one thing I knew for sure was that I had to go back to 1927.

The kettle whistled, and I filled the pot, set the lid over the brewing tea, and carried the tray up to the library.

"Brianna," I said, as I set the tray down on the end of the table.

Brianna looked up. Then her brows drew together. "Why are you dressed like that?"

I looked down. I had almost forgotten that I had changed my clothes.

That was awfully convenient. Was it too convenient? Was fate trying to steer me around?

But this was no time for paranoia. So far as I knew, nothing we did affected the weather, so I should just chalk that up to coincidence.

"I need to get back to 1927," I said. "You can do it alone, can't you?"

"I can, now that Sophie and I have tinkered with the integrity of the portal itself," Brianna said. "I'm not sure it's a good idea."

"I still need to walk," I said, and Brianna looked at me with deep confusion. "It's raining outside," I said, pointing to the window behind her. The glass was being pelted so hard with gigantic drops of rain it was impossible to see the tree just a few feet away.

"Oh," Brianna said. "You think it will be sunny in 1927?"

"Not just that," I said. "I'd like to see Mr. Thomas again."

"I think that would be nice for him," Brianna said. "He's missing his wife so much."

"You and Sophie are both working so hard, it's the least I can do," I said. "Plus, I'd like to talk to his servants. I mean, everything we really know about Mr. Brown came from Edward talking to the workers in the kitchen, and we never did that with the Thomas house."

"Oh, yes, I see," Brianna said. "That's why you're dressed that way. You look like a member of their social class, I guess."

Ugh. Another point for fate, I guess.

"Yes," I said, as if that had been my thinking all along. The table was between us so she couldn't see my period incorrect footwear. "I hate to disturb you, but it will just take a minute."

"Of course," Brianna said, then finally noticed the tray I had brought with me. "Hey, tea! Thanks for that."

"No problem," I said.

We went down the back stairs to the solarium, but Brianna caught my arm before I could march back out into the pouring rain.

"Hold on," she said, whispering a word and raising her arm up over her head. I didn't see any change, but she smiled in a satisfied way and linked her left arm through mine, still holding her wand high with the right.

We stepped out into the rain, but not a drop of it touched us. I looked up and saw it spattering against and running down the surface of some invisible barrier like a force field. Warm, dry air circulated around us, drying my soaked shoes.

"Nice spell," I said.

"Thanks," Brianna said. "Like I said, most of my spellwork is small, handy things. Like magic umbrellas."

We walked to the center of the orchard. Brianna had to dismiss her magic umbrella to use her wand to open the portal, but the trees protected us from the worst of the rain.

"I'll come back out and open this up again at sunset," Brianna said. "Will that be enough time?"

"Perfect," I said. "Just don't forget about me."

"Of course not," Brianna said, then smiled a mischievous smile. "Say hi to Edward for me."

"I will if I see him," I said.

"Oh, I'm sure you'll see him," she said.

Then she waved her wand and spoke a few words. I blinked, and the rain turned to bright, warm sunshine.

I was back in 1927.

CHAPTER 24

It was indeed another warm, sunny day in 1927. I looked up at the empty house for a moment, still curious whether it would ever be possible to bump into Miss Zenobia in the past. But now wasn't the time to test that theory. I followed the stepping stones around the side of the house to the front walk and set off for the Thomas house at a brisk pace.

I kept my head down, but I still caught people noticing the shoes on my feet, the star logos prominent on the ankles in an age where no one wore that sort of thing. A few shot me an odd look, but no one said a word.

When I got to the Thomas house and ran up the steps to knock on the door, I realized that wouldn't be necessary. The door was standing halfway open, creaking back and forth gently in the breeze. All the curtains were still pulled close, and I could see nothing but darkness beyond that door.

"Hello?" I called, giving the door a little tap with my knuckles. I would think someone wanting fresh air on a warm day would start with those windows, but I didn't want to make any assumptions.

Then I heard someone answer my greeting. I couldn't make out any words, just a little grunt of voice.

I didn't like the sound of that grunt.

"I'm coming in," I announced, and pushed the door fully open.

And saw Frank Thomas desperately trying to crawl towards me, one hand raised imploring. Blood dripped in little rivers down the sides of his face.

I ran forward, falling to my knees beside him just as whatever energy he had managed to summon abandoned him.

"What happened?" I asked as he labored for breath in my arms. I touched the top of his head, and my fingers grew sticky with blood.

Then I touched the back of his head and felt the sunken place, so like the one on the back of his late wife's skull.

"Mr. Thomas! Who did this to you?" I asked. He looked up at me, his mouth working but not forming words. His voice was only a whistle of breath until that too died away.

His eyes stayed locked on mine for a moment after his breath failed. I think there was something like relief there, that he hadn't died alone. I found his hand and squeezed it tight until the light left his eyes.

I laid him gently back down on the floor, but my hands were shaking. Not with grief, and not with fear.

I was angry. I didn't even know it was possible to feel so angry.

I was angry at whoever did this, sure, but mostly I was angry at myself for being too late.

The feeling that I had always relied on to guide me to where I needed to be in the nick of time had let me down. If it had come in the morning when it was supposed to, I would have been with Frank since breakfast. I could have prevented this.

But the feeling had come too late. I had come too late.

There was nothing I could do with the anger I felt towards, I guess, the fickleness of fate. But the anger I felt towards the murderer? That I could direct to good use.

I got up from the floor, wiping my hands down the front of my dress, and headed for the kitchen.

"Hello?" I called, less friendly this time. "Is anyone else still in this house? No need to hide now."

Surely, whoever had done this had fled out the front door, but someone else should have been home at the same time. If Molly had done it, then Helen might be lying dead or dying on the kitchen floor even now. If someone else was to blame, it might be the maid bleeding out on the floor.

The only way to know was to go into the kitchen.

I pushed open the door and looked inside. Broken crockery covered the floor, dusted over everywhere by spilled flour and sugar and tea.

But there was no sign of another body.

There was no way to step inside without leaving very distinctive footprints in all that flour. I leaned as far into the room as I could, craning my neck to see all the way back to the pantry, but whoever had done this damage was gone.

All the crockery smashed. Had they been looking for something? Something hidden in the sugar or the flour?

I glanced up at the hutch, but nothing lurked atop it.

It looked like the culprit had even searched the ice box. The door hung open, just as the front door had. The food had been pulled out and left piled up on the floor in front of the appliance.

The marble holder for the marble rolling pin sat empty, still inside the icebox.

My eyes scanned that pile of food over and over, but I was quite certain it wasn't large enough to conceal that rolling pin.

You know, the heavy, long, narrow object that would make an injury just like the one on both of the Thomases' heads.

If I was right, if that had been the murder weapon, both it and the amulet were now gone. A smart murderer would even now be destroying them both to cover up the crime.

Unless they knew what the amulet did. In that case, they could be heading back to 2018 even now.

2018, where Sophie and Brianna were both so engrossed in what they were doing, they wouldn't notice someone creeping up to them unless that person called their name. Maybe not even then.

I had to get back. My friends were in danger.

I pushed away from the doorframe, running down the long hallway to the bright light beyond the front door. I had to jump over Frank. I hoped he wouldn't mind. I think he would have understood, or at least would have believed whatever I did was necessary even if he didn't understand it and had given me his full support.

He hadn't deserved to die this way.

I burst out of the front door, leaped off the porch to land in the lawn and tore off down the sidewalk, suddenly very happy I had worn my sneakers.

I remembered how Frank's skull had felt under my fingertips. He hadn't lived long after that blow. Whoever had done it had just missed bumping into me on my way to the house. For all I knew, I had passed them on the sidewalk and not known.

I pushed for extra speed. I had spent too long in that house before I had figured it out, but I still might get back in time to stop whoever it was from using the amulet. They had walked normally, not wanting to draw attention.

I was running full out, ignoring the stares and even the cries of alarm as I barrelled past pairs of lovers out for a stroll, nannies pushing babies in prams, men in tall hats going about their terribly important business.

I thought I heard a voice as I reached the charm school, someone in the backyard speaking.

Then another voice answered, and my whole body shuddered. I felt suddenly acutely ill, like everything inside me cramping up at once. I tripped over my own feet and stumbled against the front corner of the house, clutching the brick as I tried to catch my breath. Every inhalation sent a fresh wave of cramps all through me. What was happening to me?

Then the voice stopped, and I could breathe normally again.

If I had taken a moment to think about it, I might have been reluctant to continue on to the backyard. I might have thought twice about confronting the owner of a voice so dripping with malice it made me physically ill.

But I didn't take time to think. I pushed off the corner and back into as much of a sprint as my legs could manage.

When this was all over, I was going to get back on track with the exercise thing.

I thought I saw a flash, but a weirdly timed flash. It lit up the world while my eyes were closed in a blink and was gone by the time they were open again.

Then I was in the backyard. The completely empty backyard.

I had been too late.

And now there was nothing I could do. Brianna wouldn't be back for me until sunset, and that was hours and hours away.

The murderer, the murder weapon and the amulet all were in 2018 now.

And the murderer, I just knew in my bones, was there to kill the two of them. I still didn't know if it was Helen or Molly, but whichever, they would have to come back for me. Assuming that I, with no powers to speak of, mattered at all.

My friends were in danger, and there was nothing I could do to save them. No way I could warn them.

I was stuck in the wrong decade at the wrong time.

I don't know how long I stood there, just gaping like a dummy. Probably not all that long, because the moment the stitch in my side made itself felt I instantly was fighting to get my breath back.

So out of shape.

But it wasn't just the sprinting. I still had all that anger in me, and frustration at being locked out of my own house (so to speak), and just the knowledge that I had failed as utterly as it was possible to fail.

So I think what I was really doing was pacing around and hyperventilating rather than getting my breath back. That's probably why Coco and Edward had such alarm on their faces when they popped around the corner to see what all the fuss was about.

"Were you shouting back here?" Coco asked, looking around for any other possible culprit.

"The murderer," I said between painful gasps. I made a fist and pressed it to my side. That helped a little. "They were just here. I *just* missed them."

"Which way did they go?" Edward asked, rising up on his toes. I didn't doubt he was prepared to run all the way to the river if he had to.

"No good," I said, shaking my head. "They are well and truly gone."

"But you know who it is?" Edward asked.

This time I just shook my head.

"Then how did you..." but he broke off with a frustrated sigh. "Perhaps you had better explain from the beginning."

"Perhaps I should just show you," I said, and brushed past the two of them to walk back to the Thomas house.

Coco trotted to catch up, falling into step beside me. She looked down at my feet. "I like your shoes," she whispered.

"Where are Brianna and Sophie?" Edward asked as he fell into step on the other side of me.

"At the school, preoccupied with other things," I said. "I know we can't get the police to investigate Cynthia's murder since the body isn't here—"

"The body isn't here?" Edward said. "Where is it?"

"Not important," I said. "The important thing is there is a body now. Same murderer, same murder weapon. Now when you call them, they'll have to investigate."

"Who died?" Coco asked.

"Frank. Mr. Thomas," I said. "Maybe someone else as well. Helen, or Molly the maid. I didn't search the whole house."

"This is crazy," Edward said. "I mean, crime happens all the time where I grew up, but in this part of town, everyone's too posh for such petty acts of violence. They like to keep their crime confined to their accounting books."

"If they buy alcohol for their posh parties, they are participating in the violence," I said.

"Oh sure," Edward agreed. "But this is different."

"It is at that," I said. "Coco, maybe you should stay out here."

Coco opened her mouth to argue, but Edward cut her off. "Yes, stay out here and wave down the police when they come. But don't leave! We might need you to run some other errands for us."

"Okay," Coco said. I could tell she was trying to sound sullen, but the possibility of being assigned tasks in the investigation of a murder had her practically glowing with pride and excitement.

The door had swung back to its half-open, half-closed position. I pushed it back against the wall and looked inside before stepping into the darkness. Edward followed beside me, taking off his hat as he crossed the threshold as if out of ingrained habit.

"Oh, Mr. Thomas," he said with genuine sadness when his eyes had adjusted to the semidarkness enough to see the old man still laying on the floor.

"The kitchen has been ransacked," I said, pointing at the door. Edward crept past Frank to investigate, and I stepped into the parlor.

Nothing seemed to have occurred in this room. It was just as it was the last time I had been inside. A cup half-filled with tea sat primly on the little table beside Frank's favorite chair. His gray wool lap blanket lay draped over the opposite arm as if he had just set it aside to rise.

Someone had called to him, had lured him out into the hall before striking. That anger roiled in my belly some more.

Then my eyes fell on the fold of paper tucked under the saucer. I gently tugged it out from under the tea and unfolded it.

It was the telegram from Mr. Trevor informing him of Cynthia's death.

The telegram Mr. Trevor had sent via a certain Tabitha in London. Tabitha, the time traveling witch.

"I need to send a telegram," I said to Edward when he appeared at the parlor door.

"All right," he said doubtfully.

"Did you call the police?" I asked.

"I have," he said. "I looked around upstairs, but no sign of Helen or Molly. But you should go. I think it might be better if you weren't here when the cops arrive. The cops don't really like the charm school. They might give you trouble."

So the criminals of prohibition era St. Paul kept their affairs far from the charm school, but law enforcement had a grudge against them? Just what had Miss Zenobia Weekes been up to in 1927?

"Where can I send a telegram?" I asked, holding up the paper as if that explained why I needed to know.

"Coco can show you," Edward said. "She's waiting out front. You should hurry."

"Right," I said, tucking the telegram in the pocket of my dress. "Thank you so much. For everything."

He nodded, still distracted by Frank laying so near to him, but when I moved to pass him in the doorway, he caught hold of my arm. I stopped to look up at him, all too aware of how close our faces were, how his body was so near to touching mine that I could feel his warmth.

"Be careful," he said. "If you're right and that murderer gave you the slip in your own backyard, even the school might not be safe."

"I'll be careful," I promised. I caught hold of his hand on my arm and gave it a squeeze before slipping away from him.

"I hear the car coming," Coco said as I hopped down the steps.

"Come with me, quickly," I said, taking her hand. "Apparently I can't be caught here."

"No, the coppers really don't like you students," Coco agreed, and we walked as quickly as we dared down the sidewalk, away from the Thomas house. "Do you think I might be able to attend soon? I asked last year, but Miss Zenobia said I was too little."

"I'm afraid that's up to Miss Zenobia," I said. I had no idea what the admission requirements were. "I need to send a telegram. Can you help me?"

"Oh, sure," Coco said. "We should probably be walking the other way, though."

"We'll go around the block," I said. I didn't want to look suspicious, suddenly changing direction, and I really didn't want to risk walking in front of the Thomas house just as Edward was showing the police officers the crime scene.

But walking all the way around the block and then back up to Summit Avenue was maddening. I wasn't wearing a watch, but I felt every tick of every second, like it was a grain of sand in an hourglass.

And I was running out of sand.

"Here we go," Coco said, pulling me towards a small office between a tobacco store and a corner market. "Mr. Gates. We need to send a telegram."

"It's urgent," I said to the balding man behind the counter.

"Most telegrams are," he said. I bit down on my lip and contained the anger/frustration/insanely strong desire to scream that kept building up inside of me. It only appeared like he was taking far too much time fetching out the little form and checking the sharpness of his pencil before looking up at me.

"Can I just write it?" I asked in a rush of impatience.

"If you like," he said, sliding the form and pencil over to me. I started scribbling at once. "It won't be confidential, you know. I have to read it in order to send it."

"That's fine," I said, pushing the form back, along with the telegram from Tabitha. "You can send it back to this woman, can't you?"

"It will be the overseas rate," Mr. Gates said and looked up at me expectantly.

"That's fine," I said, but he still just stood there blinking at me.

If I had known any magic, in that moment I'm certain I would have turned him into a newt.

"Charge it to the school," Coco hissed at me, and I realized what the hangup was. I patted the pockets of my dress, but I was indeed without any sort of cash.

"Can you?" I asked, giving him a pleading smile. "Miss Zenobia Weekes' Charm School for Exceptional Young Ladies."

"I'll add it to the account," Mr. Gates said as if this were the most ordinary thing in the world.

And perhaps it was. I had so much left to learn.

"Now what?" Coco asked, bouncing on her toes as we emerged back out onto the sidewalk.

"I should get back to the school," I said.

"Oh," Coco said, clearly disappointed. Had she thought I was going to bring her with me on some foot chase of the murderer?

But a group of her friends was waiting on the sidewalk outside of her house, all in a tizzy about something some boy had said to one of the other girls. They all seemed desperate to get Coco's opinion on what this boy had meant and what the girl should do about it.

I slipped away, quite ignored by all of them.

There was a little bench in the backyard between the flowerbeds and the orchard. I sat down on it and rested my chin in my hands. Either the telegram would get through, and someone would open the portal at any moment, or it wouldn't, and I would be stuck waiting here until sunset. There was nothing else I could do to influence anything.

All I could do was wait.

I hated waiting.

Suddenly, the world around me seemed to acquire a sort of gleam, like everything had its own silvery halo. I looked up at the tree branches over my head and at the deeply indigo sky beyond. I saw silvery ribbons dancing across that sky, points of light bursting like tiny fireworks all around.

Had I been drugged somehow?

I was still staring up at the sky when the effect faded. The blue was all gone, nothing but puffy gray clouds scuttling quickly beneath a darker layer of slow-moving cloud.

I was back in my own time.

I was also completely alone. I had seen the transition that time. It had been indescribably beautiful. But who had opened the portal for me? There was no sign of Brianna or of Sophie.

A breeze rustled the tree branches, and a cascade of water droplets shook down over me, running coldly down the back of my dress. I got up from the bench and ran inside, stopping just inside the solarium door to shake the back of my dress and wipe off the bottoms of my feet.

A shadow fell over me, and somehow I just knew instinctively that this wasn't a darker cloud blotting out the sun. I flinched, tucking my head down between my shoulders.

I guess that little flinch saved my life.

CHAPTER 26

I mean, I still got hit in the head. But rather than taking the blow square on the back of the skull, the rolling pin grazed past my temple.

And by graze, I mean sort of bounced off the bone with a nice loud crack right in my ear.

So when I tell you that my brain really, really wanted to just black out and go away for a little while, you'll know it's not because I'm a wimp.

It didn't even really hurt at first. It was a shock and surprise, and then the floor sort of rushed up at me and I realized I was on my knees now, and something dark was spotting the floor and the back of my hand.

I focused on those dark splotches as they multiplied by twos and threes, and I was really confused what was falling out of the sky to stain the floor like that.

The floor that was tilting underneath me like the deck of a ship on high seas, only not so regularly pitching back and forth.

I kind of wanted to throw up as well, and the first inkling of terror I had was the idea that I would do both simultaneously, puke and blackout, and then I'd choke and die.

I didn't want to die.

I didn't realize there was a buzzing in my ears like a swarm of bees until it faded enough for me to hear something else. A voice. One of the voices I had heard speaking in the backyard in 1927, only thank goodness, not the truly evil one.

Although the disdain dripping from this voice was giving that one a good run for its money.

"Can't get up? No will to fight? I thought you were a witch. I thought you were *exceptional*."

I looked up over my shoulder. Moving my head brought a fresh wave of nausea, and I nearly did pass out. It took a long moment for the blackness to recede from my vision, for the tunnel to open wide enough for me to see who was towering over me, bloody rolling pin in hand.

Helen.

"Why?" I croaked.

"Why? Isn't that obvious?" Helen asked with a hysterical laugh. "I know all about this place. I know all of its secrets."

"Doubt that," I said. It was a strain to keep my head turned like it was, but I was afraid if I looked away I'd be lost to that vertigo again.

"Oh, but I assure you I do," Helen said, bending down to speak closer to my face. The rolling pin disappeared from my field of view. "I was a student here myself, you know. I came the same day my sister did. We enrolled together, just like we did everything together. More than just sisters, we were best friends for life. Or we would have been, if not for Miss Zenobia. No, Miss Zenobia couldn't have anyone sharing a bond she wasn't a part of. She split us up almost at once, and Cynthia became exceptional while I remained ordinary."

"That's not—" I started to stay.

"I know what exceptional means," Helen spat at me. "You think Cynthia was elevated to a position less than that, less than yours, but she wasn't. No, I think Miss Zenobia lifted her up even higher."

"I'm not exceptional," I said, but Helen just laughed.

"You certainly don't seem to be at the moment, bleeding out all over Miss Zenobia's solarium floor. No fight in you at all, is there?" she taunted.

I tried to sit back on my heels, but the world pitched away from me, and I ended up hunched low over my hands, fingers clawing as if I could get a firm hold in the flooring.

"No, my sister wasn't exceptional," Helen said. "In a way, that's worse. If she had been, treating us differently would have made some sense. But she wasn't. So why all the extra attention? Why was I pushed aside? Ignored?"

"Awfully hung up on a teacher," I said. My eyes were closed, forehead pressed to the floor, but I sensed her stiffen at my words.

"It's not about Miss Zenobia," Helen said with even more disdain than before.

"No," I said, swallowing back the rising bile in my throat. "It's about Frank."

"Frank," Helen agreed. "I met Frank first, but he never remembers that. All the stories he tells about meeting and wooing my sister. I was there for every party, every picnic, every outing. And I was attentive to him in a way my sister never could be bothered to be. And he doesn't even remember any of it."

"Frank deserved better than you," I said.

"He deserved better than my sister!" Helen roared, and I braced myself for another blow.

But it didn't come.

"It doesn't matter," she said, and her sudden calm was so much more frightening than her rage had been. "Even with her gone, he won't have me. So he's gone now. But Miss Zenobia remains."

"Miss Zenobia is dead," I said.

"Oh, I know," Helen said, still in that eerily calm voice. "But her school still stands. And that offends me."

I tried again to sit back, but I just couldn't. I felt unsteady, like my inner ears didn't know how to find equilibrium anymore. I couldn't even open my eyes.

I wanted to know if Brianna and Sophie were still safe. But I couldn't ask, because there was always the chance that Helen didn't realize they were in the house. I didn't want to give them away.

"This school will always stand," I said because I had to say something.

"Don't be ridiculous," Helen said with a barking laugh. "It's been destroyed before; it can be destroyed again."

"The house can," I conceded. "Not the school."

"You might think that," Helen said, and she knelt down in front of me, leaning in close to look at my face. I forced my eyes to open. One managed it better than the other. "You might, and maybe in most cases, you would be right. But not this time. Because I have an ally, a powerful ally who's been waiting a very, very long time to destroy Miss Zenobia. And yes, I know she's dead, but she won't be truly destroyed until everything she's touched, everyone she's ever known, is completely destroyed."

"She lived for centuries," I said, peering up at her with the one eye that was working a bit better. "You could never destroy everything she did."

"You don't know my ally," Helen said. "Well, I think we've chatted long enough, don't you? Time to be on with it."

I wanted to fight. I wanted to run, to scream, to tackle the woman standing over me.

But my body wouldn't cooperate. It was too battered, too exhausted. I had nothing left.

I pressed my forehead to my hands and waited for the blow to come.

"Now!"

Was that Sophie?

The racks of potted plants all around us exploded, filling the air with twisted leaves, sprays of dirt, shards of pottery.

Helen cried out in alarm, and her feet stumbled back a few steps away from me.

But only for a moment. She started to charge towards the kitchen but was blown back by a blast of wind. I hunkered low, letting the hurricane pass over me.

"You're no match for me!" Helen yelled. I looked up to see she had shifted her rolling pin to her left hand. She fished something out of the pocket of her skirt: a little crystal ball like the one in Miss Zenobia's office.

Only this one wasn't filled with golden, sharp-edged discs. No, this one contained a swirling mass of inky forms, all twisting and turning around each other.

And when she threw it down the hall to land between Sophie and Brianna, it smashed with a bang like a grenade, showering them both with bits of glass.

There was a sulfur smell that carried all the way to where I still cowered on the floor.

And then Sophie and Brianna started shrieking. The inky forms were gaining shape. Dozens of little devil things with sharp teeth, sharp horns on their heads, sharp talons on their hands and feet, even a sharply barbed point to the ends of their tails. They swarmed both of my housemates, biting and clawing and stinging, each wound leaving a bright red welt with a blackened center as if the tissue there were necrotic already.

Helen was laughing. And my friends were crying out in pain and dismay.

And I remained crumpled helplessly on the floor.

I closed my eyes and pushed away the tiredness, the nausea, the swimming feeling in my head. None of that mattered. I shoved it all aside and founded the one thing I really did need.

My anger.

My hands grasped at the floor again, but this time, they didn't feel helpless.

Something was flowing into me. Like the house itself was filling me with energy, coursing into my hands through the floor, from the very foundation of the building.

Filling me with strength.

CHAPTER 27

The power kept flowing into me, wave after wave. It was like being out too long in the sun and taking gulp after gulp of ice cold water. It sloshed uncomfortably in my belly, but I just couldn't slake my thirst.

I needed more.

Finally, it was like the house pushed me away and I was thrown back onto my heels, finally able to sit up.

I opened my eyes.

The world around me was all dancing, glittering silver. What I had seen when I had passed through the portal had only been the faintest hint of what I was seeing now. It took a moment to even make out the outlines of anything beyond the silver. It was like the kitchen, the house, everything had simply ceased to be.

Then I started to make out the details. The silver was a million tiny threads running in a million different directions, like a web of impossible complexity.

I hadn't understood what Brianna had been saying before about multiple dimensions. How could anyone picture such a thing? But I was seeing it now. Everywhere I looked, the points with all of their collapsed extra dimensions expanded out to fill my view. The sketches hadn't even properly suggested it. They were like a stick figure of a man, and now I was seeing a Leonardo da Vinci drawing, even more beautifully detailed than real life.

It was disorienting, to say the least.

But I started to see patterns. I saw where the threads gathered together to suggest shapes. Helen, Sophie, Brianna.

The thousand intersections that made the little devil things, all dancing in and around the other threads, plucking them and disrupting them as they danced.

I stood up, or part of me did. I'm not really sure how much of me was left back in the real world. But I caught hold of those little inter-sections of threads and started pulling, tangling the threads until they formed a single larger knot.

Then I blinked, and the world changed. I was standing in the middle of the kitchen, Helen beside me. She was staring down the hall, the rolling pin forgotten in her hand as she gasped in terror at something else she was seeing.

I turned my head to follow her gaze, down the length of the hallway to where Sophie and Brianna were sprawled on opposite sides of the hallway, one in the dining room and the other in the butler's pantry.

Between them was a single massive devil thing. Same teeth, horns, talon and tail, although now that it was bigger, I could see the poiso-nous ichor that coated each of those.

I had turned a thousand tiny menaces into one gigantic one. Was that helpful?

Brianna got up on one knee, aimed with the three fingers of her left hand, and shouted the incantation as she waved her wand at it. Her bolt of energy hit the thing square in the middle, and the smell of sulfur filled the air once more.

Then Sophie was on her feet, creating the hurricane winds once more, holding the creature trapped in the center of the hallway as Brianna struck another blow, then another.

Each one left the creature smoking and reeking of sulfur, but I could see that it was also shrinking. Its skin was emitting inky smoke as if it were losing cohesion.

Brianna summoned one last blow, then fell to her hands and knees, her energy spent.

But it had been enough. The last bolt had scattered what remained of the thing. For a moment, it was nothing more than streaks of inky cloud in the whirlwind that Sophie controlled. Then she flung it down the hall, blowing open the front door and casting the thing up into the skies.

I don't, strictly speaking, know what happened to it after that. But I could still sense the world of threads and I felt it dissipate, thinner and thinner. Perhaps it had the power to pull itself back together, but that would take time. Like, years. The three of us would be ready for it, if it ever returned.

I turned to Helen, who flinched even at that small motion and raised the rolling pin again. Her entire hand was a gory red mess, my blood and Frank's staining her skin.

I blinked and was back in the world of threads. I looked more closely, deeper into the node that was Helen.

I saw no evil, not the way I had seen inside of that cloud of blue devils she had unleashed. But I saw bitterness, bitterness she had carefully nursed into a fierce hatred. Decades she had put into growing that hate. The intersections of web that formed her being had lost all of its silvery luster. There was nothing there but ugliness now.

Still, not evil. Just a sadly misguided human.

I could feel the power coursing through me. I knew I could snuff out Helen's life with a thought. Just cut her off from the world of the living and leave her body to fall like a marionette after its strings are cut.

But it wouldn't be justice. And it wouldn't be what Cynthia and Frank would have wanted.

I blinked back into the world and realized I had tears in my eyes.

"They didn't deserve to die that way," I said.

Helen sneered at me. The anger inside of me tried to kick up again, and it took all I had to fight it back down.

To remember compassion.

Helen really was just a sad, pathetic little thing.

When I flicked my hand, bonds of eldritch light like Brianna's bolts flowed away from me, wrapping themselves around Helen until she was tied up like a maiden about to be left on the train tracks by a mustache-twirling villain.

We could do the same with real rope before we turned her over to the authorities, but for now, she was quite contained.

I felt something else calling me, like an enormous wave forming just behind my back. I turned to face it and the world went back to being filled with nodes of silver threads.

The portal between times. I could see it clearly, could study its structure. It was all so clear, and yet I didn't know how I understood it. I just instinctively knew how the portal through time was formed.

I could see which thread to pull to collapse the entire thing forever.

I could see which other threads to weave open to expand it. I could make an opening so large and stable any person, magical or not, could walk through to the past or to the present. There would be no more secrets.

I could choose. The power was mine.

Vaguely, I felt more than heard someone calling my name. It wasn't Sophie or Brianna, although I could sense them breathing, watching me from where they huddled together in the hall.

It wasn't Cynthia, calling to me from beyond the grave.

It wasn't even the voice that had called me to the box, that had tried to lure me to open it before the appointed time.

It was only then I realized that voice had not been Miss Zenobia's. I had heard her speak in her office and never given it a moment's thought, but those two voices had been very different.

The voice that had tried to get me to open the box had been the one I had heard talking to Helen in 1927. A nicer version, hiding all of its malevolence from me, but the same voice.

But this voice calling my name now really was Miss Zenobia's. She said no more, but perhaps her momentary distraction had been enough, because when I looked back at the bridge, the feeling of wanting to use all my power to do something truly epic was gone.

I might have the power, but that didn't make it my choice. Whether the portal existed or not, how potent it was, how easy it was to slip through, those were all things that would affect so many more people than just myself. How could it just be my choice?

I was starting to see why there were three of us working together to guard this portal. We would be each other's checks and balances.

I dropped down on one knee, touching the tile floor of the kitchen. I let all that energy drain out of me, back into the house, before it could tempt me again.

Then I looked up at Sophie and Brianna, who were standing in the doorway, clutching each other tightly.

I summoned a smile.

"I guess I'm a witch," I said.

"I guess so," Sophie said, then she too managed a smile. Brianna saw us both smiling and tried to give one of her own, but only managed a slight quirk to one corner of her mouth.

"What do we do now?" Sophie asked.

"We need to take Helen back to 1927," I said. "Her and her rolling pin. It's still in her hand under all that… whatever that magic stuff is."

"But without Cynthia's body, what good will it do?" Brianna asked.

"She killed again," I said. "Frank Thomas. The police already have his body and are searching the Thomas house for clues. We're going to present her to them, murder weapon and all, all tied up with a bow."

"But what about the amulet?" Brianna asked.

I stepped up to Helen. Her eyes glared furiously at me, but one of the magical bonds was wrapped around her mouth and she couldn't have said a word even if she had wanted to.

I saw the glint of a chain under the high collar of her shirt and plucked it up. I kept pulling until the silver amulet that she had worn hidden under her clothes was on the palm of my hand.

I lifted it up over her head, not wanting to try breaking the clasp. Some things only make sense in movies; why break a perfectly good chain just because I was taking it from her? It passed through the bonds as if they were nothing more than light, but when Helen tried to struggle, to take it back from me, the bonds tightened and she fell to the floor.

Sophie went to find some more conventional rope to tie Helen up with to take her back to 1927.

"You should wear it now," Brianna said, nodding at the amulet in my hand.

"Don't you want to study it?" I asked.

"Sure," she agreed. "But I can borrow it when I need to. I think on the day to day it should be yours. Although perhaps you don't need it, now that you've found your power?"

"I think I borrowed that power," I said. "It didn't feel like it was mine."

"I did recommend starting with something small," Brianna said.

"I'll remember that," I said, rubbing at the spot on my head where Helen had hit me. My fingers came with a smear of dried blood, but the gash itself had healed. I didn't even have a headache.

I had been filled with so much power, I hadn't even realized all that I was doing with it.

I was suddenly very, very afraid of what I would do if that ever happened to me again.

Afraid, but also kind of excited.

CHAPTER 28

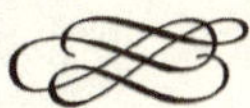

We had solved the murder; we had seen justice done, we'd even found out that I really was a witch of some sort.

We totally deserved a break.

None of us had yet gone out on the porch outside the library on the second floor, the one with all the potted trees and cast iron furniture. The furniture was a bit cold, but once we were settled with blankets and mugs of tea, it was actually really nice. The rays of the setting sun emerged from under the last of the cloud cover, bathing the porch in warmth.

It was getting on towards late September. There wouldn't be many warm evenings left.

We could hear the occasional car passing on Summit Avenue below, hear the rhythmic thumping of a runner on the sidewalk or the chatter of someone talking on a cell phone, but the porch walls were so high they couldn't see that any of us were up there.

It was perfectly lovely.

"So you have nothing left inside you at all?" Sophie asked for what must have been the tenth time.

I raised a hand and clicked my fingers. Nothing happened. I shook my head.

"But you did something before," Brianna said.

"Something amazing," Sophie added.

"I need to do more research, but we know you can do it. At least, when you're under great stress, you can," she added.

"Do not put me under great stress just to test me," I said.

"No," Brianna said, but I saw the flicker of disappointment in her eyes.

"I can teach you how I sense things," Sophie said. "Meditation to sense the flow, maybe even some dance forms to feel how you can manipulate it."

"I think that would be a very good idea," I said. "Morning meditation. Maybe a run." I grimaced at the memory of how winded I had gotten after sprinting.

That had only happened a few hours ago. Felt like a lifetime.

"You should craft a wand," Brianna said. "It really helps direct the energy."

"You'll have to show me how that works," Sophie said. "I have a wand I made with my mother, but I've never figured out how to do much with it."

"We can give each other lessons," Brianna said. "There's so much I don't know, either. We can all learn together."

"A wand sounds good," I said.

"The wood needs to be special," Brianna said. "Something meaningful to you. The closer the emotional bond, the more powerful the wand."

"I have to go back to Iowa to get the rest of my things and say my goodbyes," I said. "I know just the tree to get the wood from."

"I'll teach you the incantations before you go," Brianna said and took out her little book to start a list of things she wanted to do.

Or continue one, I guessed as I looked at the book. Her list seemed to go for several pages.

I sat back in my chair, sipping my tea and stroking the silver amulet I now wore around my neck. I remembered when I had first seen it, in the middle of a busy lunch rush in the diner back home.

If I could go back to that day, what would I tell myself? Would I give myself a warning, tell me to flee?

No, I decided. I would just say, "good luck."

I heard the thump of another runner's feet, a familiar gait. The softer pads of a loyal dog syncopated the beat. I got up from my chair and moved to the porch wall to look down on the sidewalk.

"Hey, Nick!" I called. "Nice night!"

Despite the buds in his ears, he heard me and returned my wave, but Finnegan wasn't letting him so much as pause on the way back to the condo.

I looked the other way and saw Mrs. Olson scowling up at me from her usual post at the hedge. I waved at her as well. Her scowl deepened, but then she raised a hand and gave the tiniest of waves.

"We should really look into tightening up the portal," I said. "I don't mind the music, but Mrs. Olson would appreciate if we stopped it."

"The tuning Sophie and I already did probably helped, but we can look at it again," Brianna said, then added that to the list in her book.

I settled back into my chair, snuggling the edges of the blanket around me, and took another sip of my tea. Chamomile with a generous spoonful of honey.

This felt nice. Not just the warmth of the tea in my belly or the gentle breeze playing through my hair and dropping the first of the autumn leaves at my feet.

It felt nice to enjoy a quiet moment with two friends. I had missed such moments so much since high school ended and all my friends had moved away.

And we had a calling, we three. It tied us together, probably for the rest of our lives. It was a huge responsibility, but it was also kind of comforting.

I would never be alone again.

Sophie and Brianna were talking about something, some magical technique that Sophie demonstrated with little movements of her hand, and Brianna tried to copy. Sophie made sparks with hers, but Brianna just got her fingers tangled together.

"Try it again," Sophie prompted, and made the same series of motions again.

This time when Brianna tried it, a cascade of green light erupted out of her hand and Sophie and I both laughed and clapped. Brianna flushed so red we could see it even in the dying light.

It was nice to be among friends. Even if, in little moments when they didn't think I noticed, my new friends looked at me with a nervousness that bordered on real fear.

I had channeled something massive that afternoon. We all knew it.

But I didn't mind that bit of fear. Because it was just a tiny shadow compared to my own.

Massive power. What if I was called on to summon it again? Would I be able to set it aside a second time? Or would the temptation to fulfill my every petty whim be even stronger?

I didn't know. All I did know was that I had two friends willing to do anything for me, just as I was willing to do anything for them. They would pull me back from any abyss, even one of my own making.

There wasn't a friendship in the world that held a candle to the friendship between a trio of exceptional young ladies.

CHECK OUT BOOK TWO!

The Witches Three return in Work Like a Charm, out now!

Amanda Clarke knows she's a witch. She unleashed unstoppable magic to save her friends and catch a murderer.

But she only did it the one time. And now? Back to powerlessness.

Her friends insist that all she needs is proper training. Sophie wakes her before dawn for meditation and workouts designed to channel magic. Brianna buries her under books, so many books.

Amanda longs for a distraction. But when the woman who lives next door to Miss Zenobia Weekes' Charm School for Exceptional Young Ladies turns up dead, and the murder weapon dates back to Prohibition, she gets more of a distraction than she bargained for.

But who in 1927 would want her neighbor dead in 2018?

Work Like a Charm, Book 2 in the Witches Three Cozy Mystery Series!

THE VIKING WITCH COZY
MYSTERIES

In case you missed it, check out Body at the Crossroads, the first book in the Viking Witch Cozy Mystery Series!

When her mother dies after a long illness, Ingrid Torfa must sell the family home to cover the medical bills. Her career as a book illustrator not yet exactly launched, Ingrid faces two options: live in her battered old Volkswagen, or go back to her mother's small town in northern Minnesota.

The small town that still haunts her dreams more than a decade since she last visited it. Or rather, not the town but the grandmother.

All of the drawings she fills notebooks with witches and the trolls that do their bidding? Not as whimsical in her nightmares as she sketches them in the bright light of day.

If not for her beloved cat Mjolner, living in the Volkswagen just might tempt her.

But the cat wants four walls and a door, so north she goes. And finds trouble in the form of a dead body before she even finds her grandmother's little town. How much can a town of stoic fishermen possibly be hiding?

As Ingrid is about to find out, quite a lot.

Body at the Crossroads, the first book in the Viking Witch Cozy Mystery Series!

THE WEAL & WOE BOOKSHOP
WITCH MYSTERIES

In case you missed it, check out The Teashop Terror, the first book in the new Weal & Woe Bookshop Witch Mystery Series!

No one knows more about every branch of magic than Tabitha Greene. She devoted years to studying the most esoteric texts, hunting down the most obscure source materials, and deciphering the most cryptic ancient scrolls. But her career in academia hits a dead end when no wizard will take her on as an apprentice.

Just because, despite being descended from two long and prestigious lines of witches, her attempts to actually perform any magic always fail. Often spectacularly.

But no more college means no more dorm life. And no magical skills means no real job skills, at least, not in the witchy world. And a life spent moving from school to school every few months was a life without real friendships. She finds herself alone with nowhere to go.

Then an uncle she barely remembers offers her a summer job, running his bookstore over the summer. The Weal and Woe Bookstore, located in a magical pocket world within a block of buildings just north of the old Mill District of Minneapolis, Minnesota.

Not exactly the pinnacle of all her hopes and dreams. But it's just for one summer, right?

Or so Tabitha tells herself. But unbeknownst to her, the Weal and Woe Bookstore is about to change her life.

The Teashop Terror, the first book in the new Weal & Woe Bookshop Witch Mystery Series!

ALSO FROM RATATOSKR PRESS

The Ritchie and Fitz Sci-Fi Murder Mysteries starts with Murder on the Intergalactic Railway.

For Murdina Ritchie, acceptance at the Oymyakon Foreign Service Academy means one last chance at her dream of becoming a diplomat for the Union of Free Worlds. For Shackleton Fitz IV, it represents his last chance not to fail out of military service entirely.

Strange that fate should throw them together now, among the last group of students admitted after the start of the semester. They had once shared the strongest of friendships. But that all ended a long time ago.

But when an insufferable but politically important woman turns up murdered, the two agree to put their differences aside and work together to solve the case.

Because the murderer might strike again. But more importantly, solving a murder would just have to impress the dour colonel who clearly thinks neither of them belong at his academy.

Murder on the Intergalactic Railway, the first book in the Ritchie and Fitz Sci-Fi Murder Mysteries, available everywhere books are sold.

FREE EBOOK!

Like exclusive, free content?

If you'd like to receive "A Collection of Witchy Prequels", a free collection of short story prequels to the Witches Three Cozy Mystery and Viking Witch Cozy Mystery series, as well as other free stories throughout the year, go to my website CateMartin.com to subscribe to my newsletter! This eBook is exclusively for newsletter subscribers and will never be sold in stores. Check it out!

ABOUT THE AUTHOR

Cate Martin has written stories which have appeared in *Mystery, Crime and Mayhem* quarterly magazine as well as in the annual *Holiday Spectacular* Advent calendar of Christmas stories. She is also the author of three witch mystery series: *The Witches Three Cozy Mysteries*, and *The Viking Witch Cozy Mysteries* and *The Weal and Woe Bookshop Witch Mysteries*. She currently lives in Minneapolis, Minnesota. You can learn more about her work at CateMartin.com.

ALSO BY CATE MARTIN

The Witches Three Cozy Mystery Series

Charm School

Work Like a Charm

Third Time is a Charm

Old World Charm

Charm his Pants Off

Charm Offensive

The Witches Three Cozy Mysteries Books 1-3

The Witches Three Cozy Mysteries Books 4-6

The Viking Witch Cozy Mystery Series

Body at the Crossroads

Death Under the Bridge

Murder on the Lake

Killing in the Village Commons

Bloodshed in the Forest

Corpse in the Mead Hall

Slaying on the Lake Shore

Bones by the Forest Road

Sacrifice Behind the Falls

Body Under the Café

Assassination in the Glade

Bewitchment After the Storm (available July 9, 2024 direct from me or August 13, 2024 in stores everywhere)

The Viking Witch Cozy Mysteries Books 1-3

The Viking Witch Cozy Mysteries Books 4-6

The Weal & Woe Bookshop Witch Mystery Series

The Teashop Terror

The Salon & Spa Scandal

The Bookseller Blunder

The Entrepreneur Enigma

The Novelty Shop Nightmare (available August 13, 2024 direct from me or September 10, 2024 in stores everywhere)

The Courtyard Conundrum (available December 10, 2024 direct from me or January 14, 2025 in stores everywhere)

www.ingramcontent.com/pod-product-compliance
Lightning Source LLC
Chambersburg PA
CBHW050401190726
48284CB00007BB/2380